BROTHERS

by

Linder McNeely

❖

FOR TONY FARESE -

THANKS for SHARING MY STORY -

Linder McNeely

Fultus™ Books

BROTHERS

by

Linder McNeely

ISBN 1-59682-089-6

Published by Fultus Corporation

Corporate Web Site: *http://www.fultus.com*

Fultus eLibrary: *http://elibrary.fultus.com*

Online Book Superstore: *http://store.fultus.com*

Writer Web Site *http://writers.fultus.com/mcneely/*

Table of Contents

Dedication

It is with a great, great love and much admiration that I dedicate this work to Rachel, the love of my life for over fifty years. Without you, this work would still be just a figment in my mind. For all of your typing, proofing, reorganizing, and for all your patience, I can only say, thank you with all my love and affection.

And then to Bobby, Ricky, and Jimbo, thanks for continually asking me to tell and re-tell this story. Without your interest and your enthusiasm, I might well have forgotten this tale long ago. Thanks for the memories.

Your loving husband and father,
Linder

Preface

In the beginning this book was not intended to be a book, far from it. This was a group of stories and tales from my childhood told to my little boys, Bobby, Ricky, and Jimbo as bedtime stories. As my boy's memories developed and their imaginations grew larger and larger, they wanted to know more and more about the old days. As we all delved into the past, then my love of the country, the South and my way of life as a child became more and more apparent and I was continually challenged to "write it down, daddy" before you forget it; I did finally get around to writing it down, thanks to the insistence of my children.

Since these stories were never told in exactly perfect grammar, I hope that you will enjoy them offered in a Southern colloquial manner now.

I sincerely appreciate your reading my story and I hope you can get a sense of the love, devotion, patriotic pride and faith in God that I was able to live during this time of my life.

Linder McNeely

Chapter 1

The Tramp

"Hurry up and get them chickens fed, we're ready to go to church," Mama yelled to me.

Feeding the chickens was my responsibility and I had been day dreaming this Sunday morning, so now I had to get it done and get it done quick.

I had always had my chores to do, but after Daddy passed away in November and then my two brothers, Bill and Smith, were drafted into the war, my duties and my life had changed. My two oldest sisters had already gone away to work in defense plants; Fern built airplanes, Sarah made Army uniforms.

I had watered the chickens and only had to put the corn in the feeders to be ready to go.

The family was ready to go to church and I was holding up the whole bunch.

"Hurry up, they're here, and we need to leave for Cambridge," Mama shouted to me.

Cambridge was our family's hallowed and sacred worship place. This ancient Methodist Church had been a place of refuge for all of my family going back to my great-grandmother, whose grave is the oldest in the cemetery. This old church had been home to the Pine Hill Masonic Lodge, located upstairs, and the pillar of worship for the Methodists in the community, including my grand-father, William David, and my Daddy, Howard, who was buried there last year.

Uncle Luther and Aunt Dale had come to drive us to church. There was no one left in our household who could drive a car or truck.

I would, but everybody told me I was too little to drive, no one would let me touch the car. My sister, Julia, was thirteen and she couldn't drive either. My Mama had been too busy caring for the family to learn to drive. Besides that, she said that it was a man's place to do the driving. Mama was a strong willed person with definite convictions about her home and her family. She believed that her first responsibility was to direct and care for her family according to God's teachings. This did not include taking on the duties and responsibilities that were customarily done by the men.

We all loaded up and away we went.

Uncle Luther was behind the steering wheel, with me in the front seat between him and Aunt Dale. Mama and my sister were in the back seat of the 1940 Chevrolet Super Deluxe. We had motored out the long road that took us by the wash place, the orchard, across the bridge, and out to 30 Highway or just plain "30" as it was called by some people. It was a state highway that ran from Oxford to Booneville, seventy-five miles of gravel and sand.

The Super Deluxe Chevy started shaking as it covered a long section of wash-board road, and as Uncle Luther dodged a sand hole the car slid to the side and almost got cross ways on the road. This happened all the time on this stretch of road, but it scared me just the same.

Just as the car got straight in the road, I saw a strange sight; a man riding a bicycle.

A strange sight indeed, for rural North Mississippi in 1943.

The bicycle wasn't so strange, but a full grown man riding it was strange. This kind of transportation was considered to be a kid's toy in our part of the world. We all tried to get a look, and Mama exclaimed, "a tramp, he'll steal everything we've got."

I had heard of tramps but I had never seen one. I had never seen anybody that looked like this person, either. As we got nearer I could see that the man had a beard and he carried a knapsack on his back. As we passed him it was plain to see that his bicycle had a luggage carrier with large baskets on each side, both packed full. On the luggage carrier was a large pack wrapped with a piece of canvas. When I turned and looked out the back window, I could see that on the handlebars there was a long square shaped tube that was also covered with canvas.

According to Mama, tramps roamed over the country, stealing anything they could get their hands on. They would ask for permission to camp on your land and offer to do odd jobs to gain your confidence. Then they would take whatever they wanted or thought they needed.

After the shock of seeing the tramp had passed, we knew we had to do something about it, but what? Why would a person like this be in our community? This man was probably not a tramp and certainly not a hobo, I thought. Maybe Mama got excited because there was a stranger in our community.

But on a bicycle?

"Turn around we've got to go back home, all of the doors and windows are open, we can't go on off and leave everything open like that." Mama said.

We had just passed the Puss-Cuss Creek Bridge and were nearly to Keel Spring, which was located right beside the gravel road, under a bunch of big beech trees. The shade there was so deep it made the air cool, even on this hot, dusty day.

Everybody stopped at the spring whether they were thirsty or not, if not to get water, then just to visit. The musty smell of moist, rotting leaves hung heavy in the air. The water was so sweet and cool and the air was so hot and dusty on 30 Highway.

Uncle Luther turned the car around at the spring. The crowd gathered around the spring was slow to move. They thought we were coming to get water or to visit.

As the Chevy Super Deluxe headed back down 30 Highway toward home, I knew that we would not go to Cambridge this Sunday. This was just too good to be true.

*****

I did not enjoy going to Cambridge. We always went to church early and walked over the cemetery, visiting the graves. The weather today was too hot and dry for this to be much pleasure to a seven year-old- boy. The church sat on a red clay hilltop with absolutely no shade. The summer sun blazed from the sky and made the heat monkeys dance along the ground. The dirt road ran by the cemetery and to the church and straight ahead to Riverside. A fork turned right to Uncle Benjamin's house and on down to Mr. Ed Wilton's cross-laid road. That road always was a curiosity to me. In the winter when the dirt road would become impassable, it was the custom to cut poles and lay them cross-ways on the road and you would drive over the poles instead of through the mud. This kept many vehicles from becoming mired down in the mud.

*****

As we crossed the section of wash-board road Uncle Luther managed to keep the car straight in the road, but we realized that the tramp on the bicycle had disappeared. The road was almost straight so we had no reason to lose sight of anyone in such a short distance. He must have gone under the bridge or off into the woods.

When we got home, Uncle Luther checked out the house and after deciding that our house was safe, the grown-ups sat in the rocking chairs on the long front porch trying to catch a breeze. Uncle Luther had checked the barn and the other out buildings; just to be sure that everything was safe.

I caught up with him just as he was looking in the smoke house. The old smoke house always was spooky to me. Dark, dusty, and musty, with spider webs everywhere. Just the smell of that old salt and hickory smoke was enough to give me the creeps. I was sure glad I was not looking alone because I was still frightened. As we walked back to the house, I asked Uncle Luther where he thought the tramp came from. He said he didn't know. We stopped by the kitchen to get a drink of water and made our way to the front porch.

They were talking about the tramp. Aunt Dale was saying, "I just don't know how safe we are with all of those German soldiers there, and even more Japanese at Como." I didn't know what they were talking about, but I knew better than to butt right in and start asking questions. I just listened. Uncle Luther said that they probably had plenty of guards and that he was sure that we were safe enough or the government would not have put the Prisoner Of War camps there.

How could we be safe with Germans and Japs so near to us? The whole thing confused me. Aunt Dale and Uncle Luther offered to come back and stay with us tonight, as they had stayed with us a few nights right after my brothers had left to go to the war.

My brothers, I wonder where they are today.

*****

Long before my brothers went away to fight in the war and before all of these changes came to my life, I would beg them to let me go with them to do the work that they did on the farm.

When they cut firewood, they went to the woods way over across the Kenny Spring Branch, where the red oaks grow. Those trees made the best firewood. At my first remembrance, my brothers did not want me to go with them because they didn't know if I could be trusted not to tell on them for smoking. After I begged and begged and promised not to tell their secrets, my brothers started taking me with them to work. What an experience this was for me!

In only a few short months I became an expert on cutting and hauling firewood and fence posts. When my brothers cut trees, they always took me to an area away from where the tree was to fall. I trusted my brothers and my brothers trusted me. I knew I needed to do as they told me to, or I would not get to come with them again. What a great team; my brothers and me. In my mind "We" were the greatest. They would select a good straight red oak with few knots and decide which way it would fall, based on the direction the wind was blowing and the way the limbs were growing from the tree. After all this was figured and decided, they took me to the designated place of safety while they sawed the giant red oak down with a cross cut saw. The tree always fell right where they said it would. I was firmly convinced that there were no other men in the world who could saw a tree down as expertly as my brothers and me. I felt secure about being there with them and helping them with their work and they always took good care of me.

*****

Mama told them we could make out; we might need them later.

We sat down for supper; Mama, my sister and me. Mama told us about the German Prisoner of War Camp at Camp McCain, near Grenada and she had heard they were getting some Japanese prisoners at a camp being built on the other side of the new reservoir close to Sardis, at a place called Como.

All this talk scared me. What did the tramp have to do with all of this talk about the Prisoner Of War Camps?

I kept thinking about the tramp and all of the things that had happened today. None of them made any sense. Maybe Mama was suspicious because the tramp had showed up today. Maybe there was really nothing to worry about except this feeling of being nervous about any new person in our community, especially one riding a bicycle.

Chapter 2

Secrets And Hideouts

Several days had come and gone, and the excitement of our encounter with the stranger had passed. My life settled into a pattern of long, hot summer days, with chores to do and not much else.

It was not yet time for cotton picking and the start of school was still a month away. There was some talk of a protracted meeting at Cambridge, but it too, was still a long way off.

I made a decision!

I would walk along our road and then follow the hot, dusty, dry ribbon of a road that ran from Oxford to Booneville.

I would visit my friend Gracie; Gracie Wilson.

Yes, my friend was a girl. Of course she was just a friend, but a friend that I had a lot in common with. We had started to school together in the first grade, and shared all the experiences of the one room school; Gracie, me, and Richard Johnson made up the entire first grade.

All the other kids in school lived in the opposite direction from us and they all walked together to school, so Gracie and I walked to school together. We had picked cotton together and we did go to the same church.

When I got to Gracie's house, her Mama gave me some cookies and some cool water from the spring, Keel Spring, the same spring where we had seen the tramp on 30 Highway.

As soon as we could wolf down our cookies, we took off to the barn to saddle Gracie's mare. Gracie spoke in a quiet voice, "I have a surprise to show you but you have to promise not to tell anybody."

I just looked at her and she said, "you have to promise not to tell."

"Ok I promise, what is it?"

"Cross your heart and hope to die?" she asked.

"Yeah, sure, what is it?"

She continued to saddle the mare and smile.

What in the world could Gracie have to show me?

We both climbed on the mare and began our ride. She just let the mare amble along the path, and up the hill toward the old Ray place.

As soon as we were out of sight of the house, she began to tell me about a strange new place that she had discovered.

Gracie guided the mare onto a trail that turned off to the west of the path that led to the Ray place. The trail cut across the brow of the hill before descending into a shaded cove where the sweet gum trees provided a canopy that completely cut off the sunlight. The shade was so deep that it would make you forget about the summer heat. After we had gone about a half a mile, we turned back in a direction that I had never been before.

"How did you find this place?" I asked. She told me that she had followed her dog, Trixie, to this place.

"Ssshh", she said and made a gesture for me to be quiet. "We are near the secret place, you have to be quiet."

Gracie stopped the mare and we both jumped off at the same time. I could not wait to see what secret she had to show me. She tied the mare in a clump of cedars and honeysuckle that gave some cover for the mare as we went further on foot. We walked slowly and silently with her leading the way.

My heart was beating so fast!

What was this big secret, anyway?

We walked a short way into a small hollow where the pine trees were growing together, with cedars and honeysuckle, making it almost impossible to walk into this almost hidden spot. To my complete surprise, there was a cabin.

This pole cabin was made from small pine trees that had been cut off and stuck in the ground. They were tied together with honeysuckle vines, making a woven wall. The cabin had only a piece of green canvas for a roof. There were no windows.

Gracie made a gesture with her finger over her lips for silence.

She walked quietly over and looked behind the cabin and around the other side. She seemed satisfied that we were alone. She asked in a whisper. "Do you want to go inside?"

I started to move to the front of the cabin, scared to death of what I might find.

She caught my arm and stopped me.

I was very glad.

I was so scared I could not move and my mouth was too dry to say a word, but I did not let her know how scared I was. I re-gained what little courage I had and started inside the little hut.

Gracie caught my arm again and motioned for me to come in the other direction. Again, I was glad Gracie had stopped me.

We slipped quietly back to where we had left the mare. We were both very scared and we agreed we would come back another time. Gracie mounted the mare and I climbed up behind her and we eased out of the cover and went back the same way we came.

We did not speak until we had gone about half the distance back to the barn. When I finally decided it was safe to talk, I asked her if she was still scared.

She said she was so scared she had goose bumps and this was a very hot July day.

Gracie stopped the mare in a small meadow and tied the reins to a sapling, to let her graze. This gave us time to talk.

My first question was:

"Whose hide-out was this?"

"How did you find it anyway?"

"How long had she known about the cabin?"

"Wait" she said, "not so fast."

"Who else knows about this place?" I asked.

After we had both caught our breath and our emotions calmed down, she explained; about two weeks ago she had been walking past the barn with her dog Trixie. Trixie had, as most dogs will do, run off in several different directions, being curious about the different smells. Trixie seemed to pick up a scent on the trail and away she went, almost like she was on the trail of a rabbit. Gracie had followed her without realizing she was being lead to a secret hide-away, belonging to nobody knows who.

When she reached the secluded spot she was surprised to discover a half-finished, crude cabin. It only had walls on three sides and no roof. To her complete surprise, she saw a bicycle partially hidden behind the cabin. The bicycle was almost completely out of sight as if it had been hidden there on purpose.

Gracie admitted that she was very scared.

She looked around to be sure she was alone. There was no one in sight. She decided to leave.

She grabbed Trixie and began to back away slowly. She finally reached the path to the trail. She began to run as fast as she could. She had to hold onto Trixie so that she would not run away and return to the mysterious hideout.

Gracie wondered who had built this little cabin. Who would build it so far from the road, unless they were hiding?

What would they be hiding from? And, why the bicycle?

All of these questions she had kept to her self. She had waited to share her secret with me.

We sat and thought about the cabin and the bicycle and what it all meant. Until today Gracie had not returned to the hut. It was as if she really expected it to be gone as if it was a dream.

But, it was not a dream, it was real. The cabin was real and the bicycle was real and there had to be a connection to the bicycle that I had seen on 30 Highway. If only I had paid more attention to the bicycle on that not-so-long-ago-Sunday. Could it possibly have been the same bicycle that we saw the tramp riding on our way to Cambridge?

It was just a bicycle. It did not get my full attention. But, the man who was riding it did.

Who was he?

How old was he?

Where did he come from?

In my effort to make some sense out of all of this, I had told Gracie about the tramp on the bicycle on 30 Highway. In our minds we had decided that the squatter who had built the cabin had to be the same person that I had seen on the bicycle, the tramp.

Gracie and I talked and tried to reason things out until it began to get late.

Late!

I was supposed to have been home long ago, to do my chores. We both agreed that we would tell no one about any of this.

I ran most of the way home, stopping only to catch my breath and wipe the sweat out of my eyes.

I had kicked up a dust as I ran down 30 Highway. The road was deserted, except for the milk truck from Rocky Ford making the return trip from the dairy in Oxford. It passed me just as I was moving onto our road.

The sweat running down my dusty legs made muddy streaks all the way to the bottoms of my bare feet.

The thought of the bicycle behind the pole cabin kept coming back to my mind.

Was this the same bicycle that I had seen the tramp riding near the spring?

It had to be.

Was it possible? Did the bicycle at the cabin have a luggage carrier and side baskets?

I stopped at the bridge. I had to know.

If it were not so late I would go back and maybe, just maybe, I could tell if the bicycle was the same one I had seen ridden by the tramp on a Sunday not too long ago.

This whole idea was crazy!

It would take at least an hour to go all the way back to the cabin and then there was only a chance that the bicycle would be at the cabin. And there is a great chance that I might get caught by the bicycle's owner.

The sun was getting low in the summer sky. It would be a week or longer before I could go back to visit Gracie.

As I caught my breath, I could hear Mama calling my name.

I knew then, that my decision was already made.

With chores to do, I would have to wait to do any more exploring. There was no question about it, I would have to wait.

Mama would not let me forget that I had stayed entirely too late. She had strong opinions about such things as being on time and taking care of ones responsibilities, whether you were little kids or grown-ups. We had to get all the chores done before dark. We did have a flashlight and batteries and a lantern, but there could be no visible light after dark. There was a black-out regulation in effect, since there was a war on.

I thought about my brothers and wondered;

Are they safe?

Where were they?

One a Sailor; the other a Marine.

If they were here they would help me with the chores, and I wouldn't be scared. The very thought of war was scary to me. After feeding the animals and bringing in wood for the kitchen stove, I washed up and we gathered in the dining room for supper.

Chapter 3

War Time

War time, that seems to be a strange term to use. My great grandfather was in a war, he didn't make it past Richmond. He's buried there in Henrico, the Confederate Cemetery, near the Chimboroza Hospital where he died. My Daddy was in a war also. He went all the way to Flanders Field and was gassed in the Argon Forest.

But now we are in a war; learning to do without, saving scrap metal, scrap paper, and saving even tiny scraps of tin foil for the war effort. That has all become a way of life for all of us.

"The war effort" is a phrase that we would all learn to live by. We had to learn to live without many things we had always considered to be necessities, which were now rationed and just non-existent at any price. Such was the lesson learned when Mama found the need to purchase a new chamber pot. This vital vessel, used by all ladies in the rural areas, does wear out. Time tends to take its toll. Ours bit the dust and with two women in the household it was considered to be a vital necessity. However, "Uncle Sam" had a different idea of vital. After Mama had gone to every hardware store in town looking for a chamber pot with no success, she resolved that our house would have a molasses bucket substituted for the chamber pot.

Quite a concession!

And all in the patriotic feeling for the war effort.

A gallon molasses bucket, was quite a step down from the two gallon, gray enamel, store bought, chamber pot that had aged itself right out of existence. The chamber pot kept the women from having to go to the out-house at night. I could make it to the edge of the porch if I had the call of nature during the night, but it was much different for the women.

Chapter 4

Scared Stiff

The day had been really hot. Mama had me working in the garden. The work never stopped, the hoeing, the weeding, the endless list of dos had overpowered the list of dones. Julia and Mama were doing the weekly wash; they were set up at the wash place under the shade of a giant red oak tree. The sun was relentless as morning passed to afternoon with only a short break for dinner.

My favorite times of the day was morning and evening. The angle of the sun cast my shadow long and lean and gave a much larger and taller illusion. At noon my shadow was only as large as my feet, making me feel much smaller and more insignificant. And so the long day passed.

After a supper of buttermilk and corn bread, baths were done; which had to be finished by dark, so there would no visible light to violate the black-out regulations. We sat on the front porch, the coolest part of our house.

There was very little news. The battery that operated the radio was conserved, with great desperation, since it too, was on the list of items rationed, so we only used it early and late for any news of the war. The little news we did get was not good.

I was scared to death. I did not know what Germans or Japs were, nor did I even want to know about Hitler. I was scared, sitting here in the dark, at the end of a long hot day, thinking about all the things that I had to be afraid of. With all the work that had to be done during the day, I did not have time to think so much about being afraid. Now it was dark. The news from the war was bad; my brothers must have been re-assigned to new outfits because we had not gotten a letter from either of them in over a month.

The owls hooted in Puss-Cuss Bottom. One owl seemed to be answered by another call out near the wash place. It made chill bumps on my skin which had been so parched and dry only a few hours ago.

Puss-Cuss Creek separates our place from Gracie's place and with not even a footbridge to cross the creek. I thought about Gracie and the cabin.

Gracie's place!

Was the tramp there?

Was his bicycle there?

Why did the tramp choose this place to make his camp?

The chill bumps were running up and down my spine. The friendly lightning bugs lit the dark yard and the orchard in front of the house. There had not been any traffic on 30 Highway since dark, for it was nearly impossible to drive in total darkness. As the night air cooled down it was time for bed, it is just now getting cool enough to sleep.

What was that strange sound?

I was more scared than before and the goose bumps grew larger.

There was that sound again, only it was more distinct.

It sounded like the squeaking of the rusty hinges on the kitchen door.

"Squeak, squeak, squeak, THUMP."

I wished my Daddy was here.

He would know what to do.

Mama was brave but she did not know what to do. She had never even shot a gun. If the need had ever arisen, she had left that chore to the men-folks. The only gun we had was Daddy's old shotgun with its long barrel and rabbit ear hammers. It was a sturdy weapon, but my Mama couldn't shoot it. She could blow the ancient bull horn loud enough to be heard all the way to the Kinney Spring Branch to call us all to dinner, or to signal if there was trouble at the house.

But she could not shoot the shotgun.

My sister was scared of anything that made a noise.

Squeak, squeak, squeak, THUMP!

How could anybody or anything get into the house?

The back door had been barred at first dark.

Squeak, squeak, squeak, THUMP!

We had no place to run, no place to hide.

Squeak, squeak, squeak, THUMP!

If only I had Uncle Luther here to protect me, but he lived over a mile away.

Squeak, squeak, squeak, THUMP!

Mama had decided it was time to investigate the origin of these sounds.

She bravely announced, "we're going in, get the broom." She was armed with the flashlight and me with the broom.

Squeak, squeak, squeak, THUMP!

The hair on the back of my neck stood up.

My sister whimpered.

"Hush," Mama said as we started through the screen door and into the hallway.

There was no movement, no sound as we walked through the hallway, walking by the light of the flashlight. Terrified, we walked in a cluster, the three of us all bunched up, my Mama, my sister, and me.

Mama was strong and courageous and she was doing a good job of not showing her fear; she had a calming effect on Julia.

Into the kitchen!

Then the dining room!

No sound, no sound at all.

We inched into the front bedroom nearest the dining room. My imagination played tricks on me.

Was I imagining all of these strange sounds?

I think not, it was all real.

The goose bumps testified to the reality.

Suddenly!

Squeak, squeak, squeak, THUMP!

There it was again, the strange noise seemed to be coming from the main front bedroom.

Mama turned in that direction and slowly moved on, Julia hanging onto Mama and me with the broom drawn back as if I were a baseball player waiting for a fast ball over the plate. Just then I realized we were all standing beside the bed.

Squeak, squeak, squeak, THUMP!

The strange, unfamiliar sound was coming from the area near our feet!

Mama shined the light and the molasses bucket under the bed, the makeshift chamber pot, sitting in its place of honor, came into our sight.

Squeak, squeak, squeak, THUMP!

It was coming from the bucket.

Mama pulled the substitute chamber pot out where we could see. Much to our surprise, there in the bucket was a great big, black, hard shell beetle bug. As it tried to climb out of the chamber pot it made the squeak, squeak, squeak, sound and as it got to the top of the bucket, it hit the ledge and fell back hitting the tin bottom with a loud THUMP.

Chapter 5

Bad Cloud A'Comin

I walked to the back of the pasture, found the cows, and drove them to the barn to be milked. I did this every single day. For some reason our cows just wouldn't come to the barn without being hunted and driven. Mama warned me, "don't run the cows; they won't give as much milk if you let'um run."

Having my instructions for the hundredth time, I started out to get the cows. This day I was lucky. I found the herd of cows in the first pasture on the Kinney meadow. Usually the cows would be at the back of our pasture and would have to be rounded up.

I took advantage of this good fortune. I closed the gate to this pasture to keep the cows rounded up. I ran across the bottom field to Gracie's house. For days I had wanted to get a better look at the tramp's bicycle. I had to know if this was the same bicycle. It is really important to me to know more about this bicycle and the person who rode it.

When I reached Gracie's house, I called out at the door. No one came. I was anxious, I called again and still no answer. After waiting for a minute, I ran to the spring. None of Gracie's family was at the spring, either. I decided to check the barn. There was no one at the barn and Gracie's mare was in her stall. Gracie's family was gone.

So I went alone, past the barn to the trail that Gracie and I had followed last week.

I moved as fast as I could, but slowly enough so that I could watch for anyone or anything that might be on the same trail. As I re-traced the path and approached the place where Gracie had tied her mare in the cedars and honeysuckle, I slowed my gait.

I inched my way along so I would not call any attention to myself or make any sound, should there be anyone there to see me.

As I approached the pole cabin, I began to wonder if he was home.

Would he be inside?

Would he be angry that I had disturbed him?

Would he be old or young?

Who was he?

I had started to imagine that he would be old and dirty and angry.

I was scared, but I had to go on.

I had come too far to turn back now.

I stopped beside a holly bush to look at the opening of the cabin. A canvas curtain had been hung to cover the entrance.

I watched and listened carefully to catch a sound or movement of any kind before I dared to move.

Nothing!

I did not hear a sound, nor did I see any movement.

I eased my way past the curtain, without entering, and down the length of the cabin until I came to the back corner of the cabin. I checked behind the cabin for any sight of the occupant. There was nothing, nor was there anyone in sight.

I made my way ever so slowly, looking for any sign that would tell me if I was really alone there.

Then I saw it!

The bicycle; in the brush and barely visible.

He was here!

With the bicycle here, he had to be nearby! At least within walking distance.

I though about running.

I could hear myself breathing. I came all the way over here and left the cows in the pasture so I could try to get a look at the bicycle, so I'm not running.

I eased my way a little further so I could see the back part of the bicycle. There were the two side baskets attached to the luggage carrier. The bicycle was black except for the dust and scratches. Not much to look at, but I was convinced this was the same bicycle that I had seen ridden by the tramp.

No mistake about the bicycle, but what about the place where the bicycle was hidden?

There was a lot of freshly dug dirt. Not a hole, but the ground behind the cabin had loose dirt all over. It was like a hole or a ditch had been dug, covered up and the extra dirt spread out in the brush.

No time to try to figure this out. I must go now.

*****

As I turned the cows into the barn lot and started the lead cow into her milking stall, Mama asked "what took you so long, it's getting late and we've got to finish before dark."

"I had to cover a lot of ground before I started driving the cows home," I answered, being very careful not to tell Mama a lie.

*****

As I tried to go to sleep, I rolled and tumbled and tossed and turned, but sleep just wouldn't come. So many thoughts kept flashing through my mind.

There are so many questions.

What could we do to protect ourselves?

How could I ever know the answer to all of these questions?

Should I tell Mama?

Were we in danger?

Did the tramp mean to do harm in our community?

I wish my brothers were here, if they were here, I would be safe.

My brothers;

*****

So much had happened since that stormy day in April, not so long ago. It was the horror of my life.

The day had started about like all others, school had even been average.

Now I am safe, now I am where I want to be. I'm so tired of thinking about war. It's so scary.

I love to watch the clouds fly by, making their different images, but I know I've been here way too long already, but it seems like I just got here.

There! Over to the side, there's a big sailing ship just as real as it can be.

Woah!

Now there's a covered wagon; each new cloud will move and shape its own form, then change completely with the next wind.

I love to get up here and watch the sailboats and covered wagons and let my imagination run wild, it's my favorite thing to do.

I've been told time and time again, not to get up here.

That cloud is so big it looks like the dust from a thousand wild steers in a runaway stampede.

War!

We don't know much about the war except that my oldest brother, Bill left two months ago for the Marines.

Now my only other brother has got to go to the Navy next Thursday, for good. He's already been to Camp Shelby for his physical examination and he passed.

The clouds don't look like anything just now, rolling and steady getting darker.

Darker and darker!

Smith had driven Mama to town to take care of some business before he had to report to Camp Shelby for his final induction. After next Thursday, there won't be anybody left here to drive.

They said they'd be back at dinner.

Julia rides the school bus to a different school; so she's not home yet, either. At thirteen, she thinks she is really big getting to ride that bus.

They told me to come right home from school and get the cows and feed the chickens.

I had not done any of these things, but I did change my school clothes and I did get out the chicken feed, but I had not put it in the feeders yet.

I had put the feed in the feed troughs for the milk cows.

I decided that there was plenty of time for me to climb the ladder behind the barn and watch the clouds go by.

I thought I had seen another big sailing ship with its sails all full of wind but the changing wind quickly blew it into the dust from the thundering herd.

I made a move to get down. As I looked out across the orchard in the direction of 30 Highway, I thought I could see dust from our car.

"My folks are home," I said to myself.

As I watched the dust rise from the wheels I could now see that it was not our car, but instead, it was the Rocky Ford milk truck coming back from its daily trip to the dairy at Oxford.

It's late.

I had better get a move on.

I ran across the pasture and across the pond levee, up the hill, and out onto the Kenny meadow and there grazing easily, I found all of our milk cows together in one bunch. I went around the herd quietly and got the bell cow headed toward our barn, easy so she wouldn't run.

After she got going I could hear the ringing sound from her bell, it was a signal for the rest of the herd to follow.

We all crossed the pond levee and then into the barn lot. I quickly put the cows in the milking stalls and closed the head gates.

"There's a storm coming up, a bad cloud," Mama said as she and Julia came into the milking barn. They hurriedly prepared to start the milking.

A bad cloud!

I did not need anything bad, especially a bad cloud but, I could stand lots of the friendly sailing ships and covered wagons that I had seen earlier from the barn top.

As I ran to the house I could see that the storm clouds were getting darker and darker. The sky was completely covered by the threatening, rolling, black cloud in the west. The sky was like one big ocean full of waves blowing and rolling over the top of each other.

Mama, Julia, and Smith were all milking the cows so that the chores could be finished before the daylight gave way to the storm.

I did not know how to milk cows, but I did get out the containers needed to strain and take care of the milk.

The sky was black all over and the thunder was rolling in the west. I did not worry too much because my brother was here and he would take care of me.

I felt as if something was smothering me, but there was nothing, except the black clouds from the coming storm.

All at once I could hear a loud noise. Something was falling on the house. There was such a roaring noise I could not think.

My brother yelled out, "hail".

The hail was as big as the oranges we would get at Christmas. I did not know what hail was, but this storm had gotten scary.

I could hear the window glass breaking letting the big chunks of ice into the house. The rain and hail was falling so hard that the whole house was covered with water and ice, both inside and out. The steady thundering sounds of the big hailstones got louder and louder as the storm raged on. How much longer would it last?

We all got together in a little bunch, with our arms around each other.

I was crying.

My sister was crying.

Mama was praying. I just knew that Mama's praying was exactly the right thing to do, but I didn't know what we would do about the orange-sized hail or all of the water that continued to pour into our house as the roof disintegrated under the steady pounding of the chunks of ice.

We could see large piles of the ice where it had drifted, just like snow.

Another window broken, glass everywhere; soon there would be no more windows to be broken.

I couldn't stand it any longer.

I made a break for the bed. I rolled up under the bed, all the way to the back and against the wall. I was not sure that I knew exactly how to pray, although I had heard my Daddy pray lots of times. I had heard the song leader at Cambridge Church pray for so long I would go to sleep and wake up a lot later during the sermon. When I would go to bed at night, I would always say my;

Now I lay me down to sleep

I pray the Lord my soul to keep

If I should die before I wake

I pray the Lord my soul to take; prayer.

But I was not going to bed; I was hiding under the bed.

And besides that, I was afraid that God was about to take us all.

The real thing was a lot different from praying about it. I just begged the Lord to protect and save us all, every one of us, my brother, Mama, my sister, and me. That's the only thing that saved us. God did protect us and save us from this dreadful storm.

After a long while, I was missed by the rest of the family. They were calling my name. I crawled up to the edge of the bed and my brother saw me, he came over and picked me up and held on to me for a long time.

The air was lighter now and the sky was a lot brighter. The piles of hail in the yard had turned the whole yard into a winter wonderland, white as snow, except we had piles and piles of the big chunks of ice.

The air was cold, so cold that we were all shivering. I didn't know if it was caused by the large amounts of hail lying around that simply cooled the air; or if the storm had brought a cold spell. Anyway, it was too cold to be comfortable.

We all walked around the house looking at the damage that the April hail had done to our house. Everything in our house was wet, soaked through and through. Every window was broken out. The wind was blowing all the way through the open windows like we were outside. But, we were not. We were in our house.

All of our beds were soaked from the rain that had flooded through the roof.

Mama looked at the clock, fifteen minutes till four; it must have started a little after three.

Less than an hour, but it seemed like all day to me. And all of the stuff it had torn up. And we hadn't even been outside to see what else was destroyed.

The April hail had completely beaten off all of the new little leaves that had been barely visible buds. Every tree was clean as if it were winter.

The house, now only a shell, did not give us much of a refuge. Mama started a fire in the cook stove in the kitchen. The stove wood was the only dry wood that we had. It had been a month since we had the need of a fire in the fireplace and all of the leftover wood from the fireplace had been taken back to the wood pile. It was now soaked.

Mama hung some wet blankets over the two windows in the kitchen, cutting off some of the cold wind.

The dark night came faster and faster.

Smith had gone out to see about our barn and the other out-buildings. He believed that the other buildings had survived the storm since they all had tin roofs.

Taking advantage of the fire in the kitchen stove, Mama cooked a hot supper. Corn bread, fried potatoes, and after opening a couple of jars, she had a welcomed hot meal. We sat there eating in silence. We were about finished when we heard sounds outside. My brother took the kerosene lamp and went into the hallway and up to the front door.

Uncle Luther had come to see about us.

After the grownups had discussed our situation for quite a long time, they decided that we could not stay here tonight with the house nearly destroyed.

We went and stayed the night with Uncle Luther and Aunt Dale, because the hailstorm had not gone as far as their house, so we would have dry beds and plenty of room. Grandpa had built the big old rambling house for his large family and now no one lived there but the two of them.

The next day it seemed reasonable for Mama and Smith to go to town and ask the draft board for a deferment for him to stay home for a few days and get our house repaired.

We all went. Uncle Luther went so that he could arrange to get the windows and roofing material needed to make the house livable. Mama went to see the chairman of the draft board, Mr. Reed. He asked us to come back to his office in his drug store. After much talk and explanation of what our problems were, most of which I did not understand, Mr. Reed told Mama that he was sorry about our problems, but he had no choice. Tears were in his eyes when he explained, "The draft law says that I cannot make an exception even with the storm and its damage". I was convinced that he had done all that he was allowed to do. Mama understood; she probably did not really expect to get the delay but she was doing her best.

Uncle Luther arranged for the roofing material, he brought some of it home later that day in his truck. He got some friends of Daddy's and with their help; they got most of the windows fixed that day. Aunt Dale had brought dry sheets and other things that we would need in order to stay at our house that night. Mama was able to get most of our stuff dried in the bright sunshine.

In a few days the only other brother left at home would be going away to war. He spent his last three days at home, on the roof, repairing our home so that we could continue to live there.

Uncle Luther had been a life-saver; he continued to watch out for us as he had in the past, until my brothers could come home and take care of us.

Chapter 6

Eye To Eye With The Tramp

Sunday came and so did the regular trip to Cambridge. This Sunday would be different. All my family had been invited to have Sunday dinner at the Wilson's house after church. This was a special time because the preacher had been invited too. Dinner would be late but it would be good; fried chicken, mashed potatoes, fried okra, sliced tomatoes, and coconut cake. Most important, maybe Gracie and I could get a chance to check on the stranger's cabin again.

******

I took play clothes so I would not have to wear my church clothes all day. My play clothes were merely a clean pair of overalls, shirt and everyday shoes.

******

After we had eaten dinner, Gracie and I went out to check her mare. This was our excuse to get out of the house. Gracie's mare had a sore knee and her Daddy had doctored it with blue liniment, but the mare could not be ridden for another week.

We quickly headed for the tramp's pole cabin. We half ran and half walked all the way. The day was too hot to be comfortable, but we had to learn all we could about the stranger.

When we got to the pine and cedar thicket, we stopped to catch our breath.

As we got near the cabin, we eyed the surroundings for signs of any movement.

We saw nothing.

I sneaked quietly to the back of the cabin with Gracie at my side, to check the area for the bicycle.

Gone!

The bicycle was gone and so was the owner, we decided.

I led the way back to the canvas that hung at the opening of the cabin.

My heart raced.

I knew this was the chance I had been waiting for.

I stuck my head past the canvas and into the cabin to get my first glimpse of the mysterious inside.

I had to go further. The cabin was dark. I had to wait a time for my eyes to get used to the darkness.

I eased inside with Gracie waiting and watching at the door opening.

The surroundings were strange. There was only a dirt floor and a bed made from poles. The bed had a blanket spread across it for a mattress.

As my eyes started to get accustomed to the darkness of the crude shelter, I tried so hard to see it all and remember every detail. This might be the only chance I would ever get to discover who he was and why he was here.

My heart pounded, but with Gracie standing guard, I had to take this opportunity to learn all I could and see all that I could see.

As my eyes scanned the unfamiliar setting, they become focused on a large object in the far corner of the cabin that was covered by a loosely thrown blanket. Above the bed I saw a raincoat and a cap hanging from a knot on the pole, but the blanket covered pile had my attention. As I crawled near the pile, my hand moved across a wire on the dirt floor. No, there were two wires. I strained to see what these two wires had to do with anything. The wires had been covered with dirt and my crawling across the dirt floor had pulled them out of the ground.

Gracie stood watch for what seemed like an eternity, but the time was flashing by.

My mind wandered.

Where was the tramp?

How much time did we have before he returned to his cabin?

I discovered that the wire ran from the pile in the corner to the crude bed. I examined the bed and found that the sleeping part would lift up. And when I lifted it up, was I ever surprised to discover what I believe to be a radio. It was a large green, rectangle shaped, cabinet with several knobs and gages. There was a cable or a large wire coming out of the back of the cabinet and going through the back wall of the cabin.

I went back to the pile in the corner and lifted up the blanket and there was another radio, it looked like the one under the bed. There were also, three very thin books that had printed covers, but they weren't printed in English. Although, I couldn't read them, I thumbed through each book quickly.

On the back cover was an insignia I had seen several times before, the sign of the Iron Cross.

I had seen the Iron Cross in a Dick Tracy comic book, but now it was real and in my hand; it struck fear in my heart.

I quickly put the books back and put the wires back under the loose dirt of the floor.

I was sweating and I could hear my heart beating in my eardrum. I felt as if each breath is going to make me explode from inside. I eased over to the door and made a motion for us to leave. Gracie was ready.

She was shaking from fear. We were both afraid of what we had found even though we were not sure of what it meant. But, we knew the stranger was up to no good.

As Gracie started across the small opening, back the way we came, I signaled for her to stop.

I was determined to go to the back of the cabin and see where the wire went that was hooked to the radio under the bed.

There it was!

Right at the ground level and then, there it goes under ground.

Where did it go?

Right into the brush where the bicycle had been hidden. The wire had been buried and the dirt was scattered all in the brush.

It would be easy to follow the trail of freshly dug dirt as it snaked through the dense woods. The trail led upward and almost straight north in the direction of the old Ray place.

Gracie grabbed me by the arm!

"I hear something," she whispered.

We both stopped in our tracks, motionless, and afraid.

The suspense of our discovery had gotten the best of us. We stood for a long time and decided we had imagined the sound.

No!

There he was!

We both saw him.

The tramp!

He was walking and pushing the bicycle along the trail.

We froze in our tracks.

What should we do?

We were barely inside the brush line in back of the cabin. The tramp was just entering the clearing in front of the cabin. We knelt down and rolled quietly into some brush. This would give us a hiding place. Maybe we would not be seen if the tramp put his bicycle where we had found it hidden before.

We were trembling. What would we do if he came further? We were seeing the mysterious person no more than fifty feet away.

What if he had seen us?

What if he came into the brush looking for us?

He was getting so close I could see his beard and his eyes. I could see he was wearing eye glasses with wire rims and he looked old.

He was coming nearer and nearer. His shirt and pants were brown and his boots black and dusty. He was wearing a knapsack on his back.

When he stopped, I noticed he was skinny. He was wearing gloves, leather gloves like his boots. He was so close to us now, I could see that his pants had several pockets, some on the sides and a pocket down low on each leg.

All of a sudden the tramp brought the bicycle to rest in the bushes not six feet from where I was.

Why was he turning back toward me?

He stood looking, as if in a deep study.

Then he leaned over, took a long square canvas tube from the bicycle handlebar, slung it over his shoulder and walked to the cabin. As he approached the canvas door, he looked left and right then entered.

I breathed again.

Gracie was white as a ghost.

We lay there without moving until we were pretty sure that he was not coming back.

I crawled further into the woods and Gracie followed, up the trail toward the Old Ray place, far enough to be out of sight of the cabin. The fresh dirt trail was still with us. I felt around in the dirt and there it was; the wire!

We would stay in the bushes and make a large circle around the cabin. This would bring us back out on 30 Highway just past Charlie Flemmons' house.

When we got back to Gracie's house, we were hot, sweaty, scared, and our emotions were in a mess.

Her mother yelled to us, "ya'll better be careful playing Fox-On-The-Wall with them Flemmons kids".

Neither of us answered.

We went right on to the spring to get a drink of the sweet, cool water and to give ourselves time to collect our thoughts.

When we got back to the house the grownups were gathered around a table in the corner of the yard, in the shade of an apple tree. They had just opened a freezer of homemade ice cream. Uncle Luther had carefully turned the ice cream freezer, adding ice and salt so that it would freeze smoothly. Aunt Dale had mixed and measured the milk and sugar and all the other good things that go into homemade ice cream before she left home that morning. There is nothing as good as a big bowl of homemade ice cream on such a hot summer day; it is the stuff dreams are made of. It will even help take our minds off all the strange things that are going on in our neighborhood.

Chapter 7

A German Spy

When I got into bed, I was confused and frightened. My stomach had a strange feeling like something bad was about to happen, an anxious feeling like I was about to get caught telling a lie. My mind wandered and yet, I could see plainly that the drifter who had ridden his bicycle into the Keel community was in fact, a German spy.

A German spy!

I must have slipped into sleep, because I awoke with a jump.

Sure, he knew exactly what he was doing; he was only a small part of a much larger plan.

His assignment might be to find out all he could about the prison camps in our area, mainly the German camp at Grenada, and to report any information he could get and send it to his headquarters.

There was no doubt that the tramp had come to our community by design. He would gather information and come to his hideaway, then relay the findings to higher authorities by radio. In this isolated rural area he could exist practically undetected. He thought he could change his disguises and blend right in.

But why here?

Could it be because there were military people nearby at Ole Miss, just a few miles away? I've heard that the largest officer training command in the country, specializing in counter intelligence, is located there.

Counter intelligence.

What could I possibly know about counter intelligence?

Well, this was a common term in my Dick Tracy comic books. I don't know a lot about counter intelligence, but I was familiar with the term.

Chapter 8

Keel School

School!

The institution charged with the responsibility of bringing us from a state of total ignorance to the learned minds of future leadership.

School! What a word. What a thought, what a way to occupy the minds of young people. What an adjustment from the seemingly carefree days of summer. Even with all of the duties and chores and never-ending list of things that must be done, the days of summer were definitely care-free compared to the busy, demanding schedule that the beginning of school brings.

Keel school.

This one-room school was home to one teacher and ten students scattered over eight grades.

The parents of the students gathered at the school house for the annual work day in preparation for the opening of school. This always happened about a week before school started. There are the usual jobs of tearing down wasp nests, which the parents did, sweeping down the spider webs, cleaning up the dirt dauber nests, washing the desks and scrubbing the floor. The parents always found ways to involve the kids.

The school had four windows and no screens, one door and a tin roof that seemed only to attract the heat from the blistering summer sun.

What a place to be.

Even though I did not like school, I had no choice in the

matter. I was expected to study, do my work and even excel in all of my classes.

I could do it, but I did not want to spend the effort. I would much rather be able to spend this time checking out the bicycle riding stranger who was camped out behind Gracie's house.

Well, I did like to study geography and spelling.

I almost made it to the county spelling bee one time. I missed out on one word, Constantinople!

Chapter 9

Cotton Picking Time

In my little corner of the world it is recognized and accepted that cotton picking time is the most important part of the farmer's year. School is also recognized with equal importance as the director of our future lives.

Cotton picking and school required a great deal of planning and scheduling so that each would be allowed to assume its own important part of our rural life. Summer school started in August and would continue for six weeks. The start time was decided by the parents and was influenced by the timeliness of the opening of most of the cotton bolls. School would start back after the six-week-lay-off for cotton picking and go until Christmas.

Even though school had been going on for a very short six weeks, I was glad to get a vacation. Anything would be better than going to school.

Cotton picking time brought much excitement and many different emotions to the South. Cotton being the only cash crop that we had to depend on, we were all excited as we thought about what we would buy with the money that we made from the cotton crop. For the grown-ups, getting the "white gold" to the cotton gin and converting the year of hard work into hard cash was their priority.

Balances had to be paid on the land notes, money set aside for next year's seed and fertilizer; then new shoes and clothes for the family and other things that was necessary in order to survive on a farm.

There was always extra work to be done this time of the year, before the first signs of winter. After cotton picking, then the molasses would have to be made, then hog killing time, and then Christmas.

The cotton sacks had been re-bottomed and tarred long before the opening of the first cotton boll.

All able-bodied people, including neighbors with no cotton of their own to pick, many outside pickers, along with all available family members, were enlisted to help gather the cotton. The talk was always about how much would be paid for picking the fluffy, snowy cotton.

A dollar a hundred or a dollar and a half a hundred? There was no way we would ever get paid much more for picking cotton here in the hills, because the custom here was that the pickers were picked up every morning, furnished dinner, weighed up, and paid off every day, then delivered back home. In the delta the pickers were paid each day but they had to furnish their own rides and food. But they were paid two, even three dollars a hundred for the cotton in their sacks.

Cotton was everywhere, plump and fluffy bolls of the white stuff. It looks like a snow bank.

The smell of a cotton field is almost indescribable; there is a clean, pure aroma and yet a slight musty smell that hangs over the cotton fields.

In the early morning, the dew covered bolls give off a strong, pungent smell as the pickers begin their day of back breaking labor.

There is a danger lurking across the white fields, one I detested; the dreaded "stinging worms." They seemed to be waiting for pickers to look away or not pay attention.

The mornings were cool, but the afternoon sun bore down in relentless, blistering rays that were so hot the old-timers would say you can see the rays extending all the way to the ground.

The new cotton sacks had a heavy mercantile smell that would take days to get broken in, but they lasted for years. The old ones, long since repaired, were ready to go to the field. The pickers were given sacks according to the size of the picker, with the children getting the shorter sacks. The adults got long sacks, some eight or even ten feet long.

The wagon, with its special tall side planks and a board nailed on to the back of the wagon to hang the cotton scales from, was taken to the cotton patch and left at the end of the rows under a shade tree so that the pickers could weigh up and empty their heavy sacks of cotton.

As surely as I didn't pay close attention, I got my hands stuck by the burrs on the sharp open bolls or I grabbed a boll that had a stinging worm wrapped around the back side, and before I knew it, I was stung. The sting turned red and swelled to a large tender whelp. I don't think anyone ever died from the dreaded sting of a stinging worm, but it sure did hurt.

I don't know which I was more afraid of, the giant cotton spiders that wove their webs between the cotton rows or the stinging worms. The spider webs in the early morning dew looks like jewels, glistening in the early light of day.

Maybe a hundred pounds! Maybe a dollar earned!

The main thing about making a dollar for a hundred pounds of cotton is what I could buy with it; Dick Tracy comic books and orange-pineapple ice cream from Fengers Creamery in Oxford.

The sun became unbearably hot as it climbed higher and higher into the hazy blue summer sky. The heat rays grew longer and longer.

How long till dinner?

And so each day went until all the cotton was picked or most likely school started back and the rest of the cotton was picked in the evening after school and on Saturdays; but, for now I will hold out until the end of the week and I wonder of the strangely dressed-man who had entered my world on a bicycle.

Chapter 10

Wasps

It is the third Sunday, a hot, sultry day and the air is so heavy a person could hardly catch a breath as the regular ritual of third Sunday began. It is preaching day at Cambridge so we started early in order to finish all of our chores. We arrived at the cemetery in time to visit the graves before the church services started. I didn't know how I was supposed to feel about this, but I felt I was expected to enjoy it. I missed my Daddy a lot and I think of him a large part of the time. One of Daddy's friends told me I needed to remember him some every day in order to not forget him completely, since I was so young when he died.

We took the walk from the cemetery down the red sand road to Cambridge Church. It was only a short walk. We could see the church from the cemetery, but it seems so far away. The dust was deep, the air was dry, and I had made this trip so many times since Daddy was buried here last year.

The men of the church had opened the doors and windows for ventilation. The old stale air within the walls of the ancient church was slow to be replaced by fresh air. The windows had no screens and when they were opened every bug, bee, and wasp in the country-side came to check out the newly created openings to the world. The air was so hot, I couldn't tell if the hot air was coming in from the outside or if the air was so hot inside it couldn't find a way to get out. The tin roof generated heat from above, radiating and intensifying the already hot air.

The dirt daubers had built their nests in long red fingers of mud that ran in every direction. These insects could build and cover an inch a day, especially if enough damp clay and water were available. The smell of stale hot air, the dirt from dirt dauber nests, the musty old songbooks and the odors from the mysterious old Pine Hill Masonic Lodge located above the church were all too much for me. I could pick cotton, weed the garden, walk the miles to get the cows, and bring in cords of firewood, better than I could tolerate this smothering church.

As the minister made his opening remarks to the eight or nine in attendance, I could see the whole congregation. The men always sat in the back of the church on the tall, homemade benches. All of the benches were terribly uncomfortable.

The screech of the old mouse-eaten organ pierced the heavy air to the tune of "I Am Thine O Lord". Then, Mr. Johnson, a tall and lanky man with long hair combed straight back, rose to lead the singing.

When the organ sounds reached a level to his liking he came out with a series of words that seemed to fit in with the scraping, screeching sounds coming out of the ancient organ.

The organist, Olivia Jennesey, was a distant cousin of my Daddy; Mama said she didn't think she was any kin. She did come all the way from Potlockoville just to play the organ, because there was no one in the Cambridge congregation who could play the thing. She had been really faithful.

In keeping time with the music she leaned forward, then to the left, her fingers reaching over one hand to the far end of the keyboard, then back to the beginning. She lunged forward as if she had sat on a pin, then, leaned backward. She would pull the knobs and pump the peddles. She really had the rhythm, or so she thought.

Nothing the organist did could overcome the scraping, screeching sounds. Just as the organist finished one chorus of the hymn and started to pick up the second verse, she came out with a loud screech.

A wasp!

A wasp!

It's up my dress!

All in one motion she jumped up from the organ stool and onto the front bench, threw her dress over her head and started shaking all over.

She shouted, "get it off, get it off!"

The men all ran out the back door to prove their modesty, leaving the chore of wasp picking to the ladies. I'm not sure where the preacher went, but in all the commotion the children were left unattended as the women looked for the wasp. The screams from the organist continued to slice through the musty air. The wasp was not found and I was actually beginning to enjoy the service, something I don't usually do. The organist grabbed at her undergarments in desperation. I hoped she would keep looking for the wasp. Finally someone realized the children, even the boys, were still there. One old matronly woman said in a loud voice "you boys get outta here, now!" The boys in the crowd had gathered closer to get a look at the organist's legs. "Get out!" the woman repeated.

I reluctantly inched back a step or two still eyeing the turned up bottom of the organist, rather enjoying the turmoil.

Mama said, "get out now!" so I got.

Needless to say, church was over. No more for today, thank goodness.

As the car rounded the curve by Mr. Huto's house, I started to ask Mama a question, when she silenced me, "there has been enough talk for today, hush".

*****

Many years later I asked my brother if he remembered hearing about the wasp incident.

"Yes", he answered,

"I've heard all about that."

He recalled a day at church the same organist was wearing a rather large, conspicuous hat. When church was over, it had started to rain. As she ran to her car it began to rain harder and harder, all in one motion, she reached down, grabbed her dress and threw it over her head, covering the hat. Away she ran across the churchyard to her car. When she was asked why she did it, her reply was,

"These legs are forty years old, the hat is brand new."

My brothers.

I wondered where they were.

Chapter 11

Up Close

Finally, a rainy Saturday, no school and it was too wet to pick cotton. Just as quick as I could finish my chores, I would head to Gracie's house while Mama had gone with Aunt Dale to Mrs. Cooper's house to quilt.

I made the turn at the end of the first cotton patch and scampered across Puss-Cuss Creek. The trickle of water running in the bottom of Puss-Cuss Creek, as I waded across, was enough to wet my britches legs up to my knees. Then I cut across Charlie Flemmons' sorghum patch and as I ran the last stretch of the way to Gracie's house, my overalls made a screeching sound as my wet legs rubbed together. The short cut took me through Gracie's barn lot and to her back door.

When Gracie's Mama questioned me about being out of breath and wet, I replied that I couldn't waste any of my first day free from cotton picking and school. When Gracie came out we headed to the barn to look at her mare's leg and then we walked the mare around the barn lot a few times. After we put her back in her stable we headed up the trail that had become so familiar to the two of us that summer.

Gracie and I were nervous as we moved along the trail. We were not paying attention to anything except getting to the tramp's cabin. As we passed the fork in the trail that leads to the Ray place, I realized that there was something odd about the trail.

I turned and went back to the fork, and we looked closely at the ground in both directions. The trail should have been used a lot. When I bent down to look closer, I could see that the trail had been brushed clean. The trail, at first glance, appeared unused and although the rain had settled the dust, the trail definitely had been used.

A few feet into the woods the trail revealed tracks, bicycle tracks as well as shoe prints. The rain had not washed away these tracks. Upon closer examination of the area, we found that just to the side of the trail there was a thin band of fresh dirt. I thought at once about the wire in back of the stranger's pole cabin. Gracie looked at me without a word, then she reached down into the muddy soil to expose the wires, the same ones that we had discovered coming out of the back of the cabin.

In disbelief we looked at each other.

Why were these wires here?

Why were they leading in the direction of the Ray place?

There was no explanation, except that we knew that the wires had something to do with the tall, bearded person who came into our community only a few short weeks ago.

The old Ray place was nothing but a huge pile of rocks and an old house place. It was at the top of a tall hill, probably the tallest in this part of the county. Everyone I knew was afraid of this place because of the rocks, some as big as cars. The story went that there was a den of rattlesnakes in that large pile of rocks.

After Gracie and I realized that there were two places for the tramp to be, either at the cabin, or at the old Ray place, we knew we would have to be much more careful as we explored the tramp's cabin.

We eased back onto the trail that lead to the cabin. As we got to the little opening that surrounded the cabin, we were well aware that the stranger might be there. There was no sign of him at the old Ray place. I crept quietly across the clearing at the front of the cabin, then on to the back of the cabin. I wanted to know if the tramp's bicycle was in its usual hiding place.

If he was here, he left no visible tracks.

The tramp was not here!

What a relief!

We moved back across the opening and were inside the cabin in an instant.

The darkness dimmed our vision as we entered. After what seemed to be an eternity, our eyes started to adjust to the darkness. Nothing looked familiar.

The bed was there but the pile of stuff in the corner had been re-arranged and stacked neatly along the front wall next to the bed. I quickly checked under the bed and all of the material had been removed. It seems that everything that had been under the bed, radio receiver, the boxes, and cabinets had been combined along the front wall. There was an old blanket and a piece of canvas draped over this collection of supplies.

Just the thought of this person, this spy being in our community, was terrifying.

Gracie was shaking and her voice trembled when she whispered, "what are we going to do now?"

I could not answer, as I raised the covers that draped over the radio equipment. It was just as I imagined; a well organized radio setup. There were the code manuals that I had seen earlier under the spy's bed, but there were more of them. I turned through them quickly and each one had the same design on the back.

The Iron Cross!

There were seven books in all. I could not read any of them but I knew, I just knew.

My instinct told me they were written in German.

These were the code manuals for operating the radio setup. Gracie stepped further into the cabin to get a better look, inching closer and closer until we focused all our attention on the code manuals.

All at once I could feel the presence of something or somebody else.

I turned to my left.

There he was!

Just past Gracie and just inside the small opening he stood, tall as a giant.

He looked as tall as a giant!

I was on my knees looking up.

He was dressed in green khaki cloth shirt and pants, black

boots and a cap similar to the kind that mechanics wear, except it was the same color as the clothing. The bearded man had a square canvas tube slung over his shoulder.

He stood there as we looked at him for what seemed like forever.

In reality it was only an instant.

The only sound was my breathing and it seemed I could hear myself shaking.

The man's voice pierced the air,

"Why are you here?"

He spoke in perfect English. I had never heard anyone talk the way he did. Even the preacher who had gone to college did not speak with the precision that this person did.

"Why are you here?" he repeated.

We did not answer, we only looked at him.

He stood barely six feet away, standing with feet apart, hands on his hips, right in front of the door opening. He looked even bigger than he did when I first saw him. He lifted the blanket covering the radio stuff then he turned his head to look around the room, checking to see if we had moved anything, I guess. When he turned his head, I motioned to Gracie.

We both lunged forward at the same time.

Gracie went right between the man's legs and out the door.

I followed her lead but he grabbed for me as I cleared his legs and he got a piece of my shirt. I gave another push forward and then we were both free and clear.

We were both out of the cabin and were running across the clearing when we heard voices. We slowed for a minute, just in time to hear voices two sets of voices coming from the direction of the trail, the same trail that we would have to use for our escape. One sounded like a woman and the other, that of a child. At once we turned and ran through the brush heading back in the direction of the trail that leads to the Ray place.

After reaching the trail, we stopped for just a minute to catch our breath. We decided to go up the hill. The main trail held too many surprises. We ran full speed up the trail to the place where the giant rocks were supposed to house rattlesnake dens. Though the rock field and out of that area, we ran so fast we did not have time to get scared of the snakes.

The idea of being that close to being caught by the German spy made my blood run cold. When we stopped to catch our breath, I realized part of my shirt sleeve was gone.

Torn from my body!

Mama would not like me getting my shirt torn, since she had spent a lot of time and effort making this shirt. She would never believe this wild talk of how my shirt had gotten torn, even if I decided to tell her.

On up the hill we climbed. When we finally reached the top, there was a small clump of pine trees where we hid.

As we sat on the wet ground to catch our breath, we began to get our senses back. We looked around and saw fresh dirt in a narrow ribbon; the rain had changed it to mud, but there it was, big as life.

The wires!

The wires ran underground all the way from the spy's cabin to the top of the hill. After scouting around the hill for a few minutes, Gracie discovered the wires coming out of the ground at the base of a pine tree and running up the pine tree as far as we could see.

We were both shocked at this discovery. Although we had seen lots of stuff, and many strange things had happened to us, we could not imagine what this was all about.

After considering all of our choices, we decided that Gracie would climb the tree to see where the wires went. She was a much better tree climber than I, and she scooted up the tree in a matter of minutes. I saw that she was staring at something. Gracie scooted back down the tree with the same ease that she went up, and she came over to the bushes where I was waiting. She said that the wires were attached to a long slender rod, about as tall as she was. The rod was attached to the tree right at the top so that it extended upward about three feet above the last limbs. This had to be some kind of antenna, we supposed, attached to the radio stuff in the cabin at the bottom of the hill.

Even though Gracie was excited about all that we had found, we were still baffled by what this meant.

What if he tried to harm our families?

There is simply no one in my family to defend us.

Who were the voices we heard on the main trail?

How long would it be before they figured out where we were and came looking for us?

We heard a sound, ever so faint, then, it was repeated.

It was an electronic sound; at least that's what Dick Tracy said it was.

Dot-dot-dash, dot-dot-dash.

Where was it coming from?

From behind the pine tree where the wires came out of the ground, there was a piece of canvas, some sort of cover.

Picking it up, I discovered a box with a battery similar to the one in the Forty Chevy, but this battery was bigger.

Attached to the battery by two wires was a machine that looked like a bicycle, only smaller. A person could put his feet on the pedals of the machine and pump as if riding a bicycle, maybe charging up the battery.

Yes, we imagined that with this machine, powered by the battery, he could send messages from the cabin to the hill top and then he could send messages to his headquarters. When the message was sent he could peddle the charging machine and have it ready to send another message.

Send messages? Who would he send messages to?

This was really and truly a spy, a German spy gathering information.

Information about what?

The prison camps in North Mississippi, or information about the training command at Ole Miss. Then he could relay the information out to other collection points?

Where?

We knew we must get out of here. It was only a matter of time before we would be in danger of being discovered again. We had no idea how many people would be looking for us. Knowing that we could not go back the same way we came, we took off straight down the steep hill. We walked and half ran, slowing up only long enough to keep from rolling down the steep incline. If we continued on the same path we would come out on the other side of the hill, somewhere in the area of Charlie Flemmons' house.

Down, down, we went, past the rock field, past the much talked about rattlesnake den. Down almost into Charlie Flemmons' garden. We walked around the edge of the garden to stay out of the rows, but we had gotten into the plowed ground enough to get our feet muddy. As we passed, Charlie Flemmons' kids were playing Fox-On-The-Wall. They all hollered at us as we went by, we yelled back, not stopping.

Gracie led the way as we crossed 30 Highway and we followed the foot path to Keel Spring. I was so exhausted from the running, walking, and being excited, I could not drink. I just sat for a while in the cool, damp sand, my feet muddy, my face scratched and part of my shirt gone, my home made shirt, torn away.

Finally, we had cooled off enough to drink and we splashed some cooling, soothing water over our bodies and managed to get ourselves back to normal. We washed our clothes as much as we could without ruining them.

Crossing 30 Highway, going back to Gracie's house, we saw the big Durant touring car coming down the road; Aunt Dale was at the steering wheel. She and Mama were coming from the quilting party and they stopped to drop off Gracie's mother.

As soon as Mama saw me she said, "I've told you and told you not to play Fox-On-The-Wall with those Flemmons' kids, they will tear your clothes off."

After I got in the back seat of the big old touring car I didn't say anything. All the way home my mind wandered as I listened to Aunt Dale talk.

1940 Chevy Super Delux

Keel School Re-union. Late 1940's.
Photo by Mr. Doyle King

UNITED STATES OF AMERICA

War Ration Book One

No. 88373 -248

WARNING

1 Punishments ranging as high as *Ten Years' Imprisonment or $10,000 Fine, or Both*, may be imposed under United States Statutes for violations thereof arising out of infractions of Rationing Orders and Regulations.

2 This book must not be transferred. It must be held and used only by or on behalf of the person to whom it has been issued, and anyone presenting it thereby represents to the Office of Price Administration, an agency of the United States Government, that it is being so held and so used. For any misuse of this book it may be taken from the holder by the Office of Price Administration.

3 In the event either of the departure from the United States of the person to whom this book is issued, or his or her death, the book must be surrendered in accordance with the Regulations.

4 Any person finding a lost book must deliver it promptly to the nearest Ration Board.

OFFICE OF PRICE ADMINISTRATION

War Ration Book 1942

1942 GWP Made by Ford Motor Co.
Photo by Mr. David Box

The Boarding House at 1415 Jackson Ave.

Oxford Elementary School.
Photo Oxford Eagle – Mrs. Patricia Young

Lafayette County Jail 1943.
Photo by Mrs. Patricia Young

Oxford Town Square. Early 1940's.
Photo by Mr. Wendell Parks

Chapter 12

Let Down

The next Sunday after church I went to Gracie's house as soon as I could get away.

As we started up the trail something felt different. Our anxious feelings were the same, but we both had the feeling that the spy would be gone. We made the trek to the fork where the trail leads to the old Ray place, seeing no tracks as we crossed the open meadow and approached the clearing.

There was no cabin!

Plain as day, there was no cabin.

Nervously, we approached the clearing where the cabin had been.

To our complete surprise, the only things left were the holes in the ground where the poles had stood. The buried wire was no longer there. We followed the trail all the way to the top of the great hill only to find everything gone; no wire, no antenna, no battery charger, nothing. We know now that we could never tell anyone any part of this story.

Who would believe it anyway?

Chapter 13

Road House

There had been some talk of my family moving into town. With the war and all, Mama could not get anybody to help us run the farm. All the able-bodied people were either in the Army or working in defense plants making supplies for the war. Mama had already made the decision to sell out, but she did not tell me anything about her plans until almost time for the sale to take place. She didn't think I would understand. She was right, I didn't.

Uncle Luther had come to drive the car. We must go to New Albany to meet with the lawyers. The car moved quietly out of our yard and across the bridge. Not much was said as we turned onto 30 Highway. Uncle Luther shifted into high gear as we passed Keel School. The school was out for the weekend as evidenced by the mud puddles in the play yard. They had not even been stepped in. We lumbered across the flat stretch and passed the old deserted CCC Camp. The car came out of the dense section of the forest as we approached the cross roads.

There it was:

"Little Chicago!"

The most notorious road house in Beat-Two.

As we got in sight of the juke joint, Mama made me turn my head and cover my eyes. I don't really know why. I did peek between my fingers as I covered my eyes, but I did not see anything but an old wood building with a tin roof. The store had a hand powered gas pump on the side near the door, nothing unusual about that.

Once I had heard some men talking about this place when they didn't know I was around. They were whispering and laughing about the things that happen there at "The Cross-Roads."

Town folks called it "Little Chicago," country folks called it "The Cross-Roads." According to the men I heard talking, on Saturday night the town folks would come out for dancing and beer drinking; yes this is a genuine beer joint. Some of the town people also came to gamble, but mostly they sat and drank beer and danced with the local girls to Jimmy Rodgers' music, played on an old wind-up, record-playing machine. All this was by the light of coal oil lamps and lanterns.

Maybe this is peculiar behavior, maybe not, but Mama did not think I should even look at the beer joint, "Little Chicago", and I didn't.

Chapter 14

Transition

The plans were made, the papers signed, so we would move to town before Christmas.

After I first heard about us moving to town, about a week passed before anything happened, then it all happened at once.

All of a sudden our farm things were sold. The animals, the farm equipment, even the huge black pots that cooked cracklins, and even the pots that lye soap was made in were sold. By the week before Thanksgiving my whole way of life had changed.

There were so many things to do. I had been back only once to check on the tramp's hideout.

There was nothing there. Maybe I should go again and be sure.

Mama made me give my dog, Snipsey, away.

He was a lot more to me than just a puppy; he was my pride and joy. He had long, blonde hair, a long body, and short legs, and he loved me a great deal. He was blind, blind from birth. Mama wanted him destroyed when he was born, but I begged for him and his life.

She said he would never amount to anything,

I said I didn't care, because all I wanted was my puppy, blind or not, all I wanted was my puppy.

Since I had raised him, and had given him all his care, he knew my voice and he learned from me.

Outside of our little world he would be lost.

Judging wisely, Mama knew he could not survive in town.

I didn't care.

I really had bad feelings about losing my home and my puppy.

My home, the only place I had ever lived with my Daddy, my home was gone. The very same ground my ancestors homesteaded on a hundred years ago was gone!

What can possibly be worth all of this sacrifice?

Chapter 15

Memories

I thought about the big brick school in Oxford and was afraid.

The only brick building I had ever been inside of was a Veterans Hospital in Memphis, where Daddy was hospitalized before his death. Uncle Luther had driven the family up there to visit him.

The last time I saw my Daddy in the Veterans Hospital, there was a man from Missouri, Daddy's roommate, who gave me a V nickel. I still have it.

And what is a nickel worth?

Mine is priceless.

My V nickel is a memory and along with it, I have many wonderful memories of my early life.

Memories of an old black friend of our family who had said to me, as we packed up our things to move, "son, you have gotta move ahead, you have gotta be the man of the family; no time for feeling sorry for yo'self. You gotta forget them childish things." I must grow up, he was saying to me.

I have followed his advice and have reminded myself not to dwell on the past. I couldn't change it then; I can't change it now, so I have tried hard to be thankful for the opportunity just to be here.

Chapter 16

Oxford Elementary

We moved into a rather roomy house on an old street on the east side of town, where Mama opened a boarding house. I had dreaded this day with the same energy that I had dreaded the opening of school at the end of summer.

The move to town took place just as Oxford Elementary School was let out for Thanksgiving, so I did not get to miss any school. I had prepared for the worst things possible. If I could think of it, or if I had the ability to imagine it, I had decided that it would happen.

Mama took me to school, that big brick school, along with every record that Keel School ever had that had anything to do with me. Most important to me was the record of my shots given by the county health nurse, who came every year to our school to stick our arms and update our shot records.

I was reluctant to take the walk up that long sidewalk that lead to the big brick schoolhouse. I had even considered running away and joining the Army, after hearing that it was much easier to lie about your age and get into the Army than it would be to get into the Navy or Marines.

Common sense took over and I took the advice of the old black man who had at one time worked for my Daddy.

He said, "you ain't gonna get nowhere feeling sorry for yo'self. There's a lot of little boys in the world whose Daddies died and left them lonesome and scared. There is lots of little boys in the world with nowhere to go; nobody to take care of 'em, So you had better hitch up them overalls and get ready to make yo' own mark." He was so right, yes, so right, but I didn't know it yet.

So I counted the steps that led from Jackson Avenue to the big brick school. It seemed that there must have been at least ten thousand of them.

As we entered the oversized doors leading into the wide entrance of the hallway, we passed some large, glass display cases. These glass cases that lined both sides of the hall were filled with different collections of things from all over the world; but mainly from Africa and Asia.

I could not believe what a neat place this was. I stopped to look because there was so much to see that I simply could not see it all. The lady who was directing us to the principals office assured me that there would be plenty of time for me to examine all these new things; time to read each display card, time to learn the origin of each piece of every display.

There was some discussion about what grade I should be in. The school said I was too young to be in the fourth grade. I had started to school early. The rules of the country school were not very strict so I started to school when I was five years old. After all the discussion the lady in the office enrolled me in one of the two sections of the fourth grade.

When we first went to the school office, I saw that there were three ladies and a girl working there. The girl was older than me but she looked like she might be a student. The young girl had her hair platted into pigtails that hung down to her waist.

I had never been to a place where so many people were working. There were all kinds of machines, typewriters, and even a telephone.

I was assigned to a classroom upstairs on the front of the school. The office lady took me to the room and spoke with the teacher. While they talked, I was able to look around the room and saw that there were windows along one side of the room, allowing the students to look out onto the street and across into the parking lot. Blackboards lined the front and one side of the room. In the back of the room there were hangers for coats. Each person had a desk and there were several rows of desks, boys and girls all sitting together.

The teacher introduced me to the class as the newest student. After the introduction, all of the boys and girls clapped their hands and then the teacher asked each student to stand and tell their names. Those names became familiar to me and I can still recall a great many. The people who stood and introduced themselves to me that day became my friends and remain my friends to this day.

This was a new beginning that I was unsure about, but it was a move forward, a move toward growing up.

There would be no more thoughts of running away and joining the Army. There would be no more self pity, only a whole new world to be explored.

I learned that in the town school, with special permission, I would be allowed to go home for lunch. There was also a lunchroom and about half the students stayed at school for lunch. I had never even heard of a lunchroom.

Except for a few minor skirmishes with some of the town boys, who wanted to beat up the new country boy, I had no problems slipping into a routine that would make an impression on me that would last a lifetime. Oxford Elementary School would be very good for me. Field trips to the Mary Buie Museum, night field trips to the Kennon Observatory on the Ole Miss Campus, and Public School Music were only a few of the things that opened a whole new life for me.

Chapter 17

Who Lives Here

One day about two weeks after I had enrolled in school, I had gone home with one of my new friends after school to study and to play. On our way home, as we passed the drug store, what I saw in the bicycle rack on the front sidewalk was a big shock. There was a bike that looked to be the very same bicycle that I had seen the German spy riding down 30 Highway. It was surely the same bicycle I had seen hidden in the brush behind the tramp's pole cabin.

Was my mind playing tricks on me?

Were my eyes working right?

No and yes, my mind is not playing tricks and yes my eyes were working right. I looked carefully and yes, this was the same bicycle. The only difference was that the bicycle was no longer dusty and scratched. It did have double baskets attached to the luggage carrier. Someone had spent a lot of time cleaning and polishing the bicycle.

Who would do this? I looked around for the stranger who had first ridden the bicycle into the Keel Community.

"Come on," Louie said. He had walked all the way to the corner before he realized I was not with the group. When Louie turned, he saw that I was looking at the bicycle rack; looking, staring in disbelief, gazing at the bicycle.

"Come on", he yelled.

*****

Louie was the first guy I had met when I moved to Oxford. He had jumped in to help me when two of the town boys had decided they wanted to see what made the country boy tick. Actually, there were only a couple of punches thrown and after Louie got in it, the two brothers took off to their house. It was Louie who had been a friend to me when I had no friends at all.

Louie seemed to know everyone and everything. He has a lot of friends in the neighborhood. Jimmy Ned Wilson, Bill Johnson, and Wilbert Gleason, who lived with his aunt in the big house on the corner. His parents had both died in a train wreck out west. Down near the cemetery was where the two rough boys lived, who tried to beat me up. Then Louie took me home with him and Louie had introduced me to things, like cold milk with lots of Hershey's syrup added in long rich strings, until about an inch or more accumulated in the bottom of the glass. He stirred it with a long spoon until the whole mixture turned a rich chocolate brown. It was so good.

*****

"Come on, haven't you ever seen a bicycle?" Louie asked. He had come back up the street to where I was standing, staring at the black bicycle.

"Come on, we've gotta go," Louie said to me.

As a boy took the bicycle out of the rack, I stood and watched in disbelief. The boy was wearing strange looking clothes. Very strange for Oxford.

He wore a suit! Coat and knickers with a shirt and tie, and long plaid socks from his knees to the shoes, these were odd to me.

He climbed on the bicycle and rode away; riding down the sidewalk in the same direction we were headed.

He never said a word, he just rode away.

He looked to be about our age.

Hard to tell dressed in this manner, and on a school day.

As he turned the corner at the bank, he almost ran over Lillian Bost.

The prettiest girl I had ever seen.

She stumbled over the curb to keep from being hit by the strange looking boy riding the black bicycle.

Someone yelled out "why don't you look where you are going, Dumbo"?

We walked along with a whole bunch of kids.

He just rode off.

As we crossed the street, Lillian stopped off at her house. Nearby was the jail, a tall sinister-looking brick structure. Another boy and his sister stopped off at the jail. They lived with their Dad in the down-stairs; their Dad was in charge of the jail.

The numbers in the group had dropped off to Louie, Wilbert, Jimmy Ned and me. Wilbert and Jimmy Ned had walked on to Louie's house with us.

We all sat in Louie's yard. They were talking about some new guy who had moved back to Oxford after he had lived in Memphis for a year.

I did not know him.

I was thinking about Lillian Bost.

The prettiest girl I had ever seen.

All the other girls I had ever been around just looked sort of like every body else, nothing outstanding.

But Lillian Bost was really pretty.

She was in my room at school.

She was the first person I had seen when the office lady introduced me to the fourth grade class.

She had a very pretty smile and her long blond hair was like silk. Her blue eyes sparkled like the stars.

She was so pretty.

*****

Wilbert said to no one in particular,

"There he is, that dressed up guy that was at the drug store!"

That broke into my daydream.

"Where?" Louie said.

"Across yonder at the Doolittle house, he's putting that bicycle in the garage, see he's wearing that Sunday school suit," Wilbert said.

We all turned and looked without saying anything.

He walked the bicycle from the front porch around to the side of the house and into the garage.

"Who is that?" Jimmy Ned asked.

No one seemed to know.

All Louie knew was what his mother had told him. She said he and his father were staying with the Doolittle family.

The Doolittle's rented rooms like a boarding house. The boy's father was in town on business. Louie's mother had told him that the man was interviewing for a job as a professor at the University. In a few minutes the strange looking kid appeared on the front porch with a man. We took for granted it was his father.

The man wore a suit also. From where we were lying in Louie's yard near the fire hydrant, we could see him well. He was a skinny guy with a strange looking beard, with only a mustache and a beard around his chin. His beard was neatly trimmed and so was his hair. He wore a heavy type suit with leather patches on his elbows. As we were looking at them we could tell that they were also looking at us; intensely as if they were actually trying to hear what we were saying. After a long while Louie's mother called to him, "Louie come on in, it's getting late and you have to do your homework."

We went into the house and started our homework, which is why I came home with him in the first place. Mrs. Parsons came in the kitchen with chocolate milk and cookies; then we settled down to get homework done. I did pretty well in history, but I needed help, lots of help with arithmetic.

My mind would not stay on arithmetic. It wandered to the well-dressed kid on the bicycle that almost ran over Lillian Bost.

Lillian Bost, she was so pretty, and she was almost run over by some strange kid that no body seems to know exactly who he is.

He is not in school either.

I bet Lillian smiled all the time, even when she did her homework.

When will he enroll at the Oxford Elementary School, and meet up with those two tough town brothers? I wondered.

Him wearing a suit with knickers.

Reckon they can find out what makes him tick.

Her hair looks so soft and she is so beautiful.

"wake up, wake up," Mrs. Parsons softly said. I jumped.

I had been daydreaming.

I guess I was really struck on Lillian Bost.

Every time I got still I would end up thinking about what a nice smile she had or something else about her.

And then my mind wandered to the strange father and son pair.

Mrs. Parsons told me it was time for me to go home, and so I did.

*****

Mama was in the front room listening to the radio news when I got home. I did not want to hear any news.

I went out to the front porch.

I could not believe my eyes!

There they were!

Standing in front of our house!

The father-son pair that we had all seen on the Doolittle porch. What are they doing here?

I stared at them wondering what they wanted.

The same people, the same clothes, no mistake about it.

They were staring back at me, especially the father.

I suddenly felt sick to my stomach. I broke out in a cold sweat and there was an eerie feeling I could not explain.

Just as I turned to go inside the father called out and asked,

"Who lives here"?

I was scared to answer.

It seems to me like I have spent a big part of my life being scared.

I did not answer, but I turned and went inside, trying hard not to hurry or to show my fear.

As I made my way to the dining room to finish my homework, the question came back to my mind.

"Who lives here"?

There was a familiar sound in that voice.

There it is again!

"Who lives here"?

Bingo! Why are you here?

There was the same sick feeling in my stomach. It got worse.

The words the German spy had said to me when he discovered me inside his pole cabin behind Gracie's house were the same.

The clear, crisp voice was exactly the same.

There were the small beady eyes set far back in his head, but now there was no beard only a mustache and goatee.

No eye-glasses, yet the same clear, crisp voice.

Why are you here?

That question made a statement.

Why are you here? I wanted to ask him.

I am here because of you.

My brothers are both off in a far away war because of you and your kind.

Why are you here?

My Mama had to sell out our home place and move here, to this town, because of you and your kind.

Why are you here?

Who would answer these questions?

When I heard the knock on the front door, my heart jumped up into my throat.

Could he be at our front door now?

Has he recognized me from the squatters hide out?

I could hear my Mama go to the front door.

I knew I could not allow Mama to go to the door and talk to this foreigner alone.

She did not know anything about what had been going on in the months before we moved to town.

I went to the front door along with my Mama.

There he stood, close up, as close as he was the day I ran between his legs to escape with only a torn shirt as testimony to the fact that I had invaded his home. I was horrified; my emotions ran from outright fear, to a very defiant rage; the very idea of this person coming to our front door!

And, yet there he was with the well dressed kid who had almost run over Lillian Bost on the black bicycle. There he was; standing at my front door.

When Mama answered the door the skinny stranger removed his hat and bowed slightly as he asked politely,

"Who lives here"?

Mama, in a most reserved manner, replied by asking the caller to identify himself and state his business.

He was inquiring of permanent housing for himself and his son. All the time, I tried to appear indifferent about the whole affair, but my eyes seemed to go back to his, those beady eyes set far back in his head. The man continued by explaining that the room they occupied at the Doolittle residence was only temporary and since he would be employed in the community, they required a permanent home. He spoke with a very precise rhythm and what seemed to me to be very correct English, maybe the most perfect English I had ever heard. Mama quietly explained that all our rooms were currently occupied and she didn't expect a vacancy.

During the entire conversation my heart was beating wildly. Sweat popped out on my forehead as I tried to conceal my anxiety. We stood there looking at each other, the dressed up kid and me, eyeball to eyeball for what seemed like forever.

He looked straight ahead, never blinking, as if memorizing each word as it was spoken. He had a strange far-away look in his eyes. After what seemed to be forever, the visitors left. I was so relieved when they left. I went back to my homework and Mama went back to the news.

Chapter 18

Soldiers

As winter slowly changed to springtime, every chance I could get, I visited my little dog Snipsey and all of my old friends and neighbors in the Keel community.

I could not have picked a better home for my puppy. His new masters were kind to him, but each time I saw him I was reminded that I had given away the best friend I ever had, the only thing that I really ever had that was mine, repeat mine, without having to share. I had given away my little puppy dog.

Each visit I made to see my puppy made me realize that he was not happy. He had survived, which he could not have done in town because of his blindness, but he was even more confused about why he had been given a new home. He grew increasingly restless and would not eat.

My trips were limited, because of the war, gas rationing and all. Uncle Luther did not make many trips into town now. In late summer I went to stay a few days with the Williams family and my little dog Snipsey.

This would be the last time I would have the opportunity to stay very long with the Williams family and my little dog. Snipsey was very weak and died in his sleep the second night I was there.

I felt that my life as I knew it in the Keel community had ended. I decided that I would never have another pet. The price to pay for disappointment was too great, I never allowed myself to get attached to a pet again.

*****

On a visit to the Williams family in late summer, the Keel school was already in session for the Summer School, the term given the early school in preparation for cotton picking.

On this Friday we were all in school and I was a visitor and had no responsibilities, but the rest of the students were doing their classes when there was a rumbling noise outside. This was very unusual because now-a-days the highway had very little traffic due to the war and the rationing program. There were few people with the means to get gasoline, tires, and the things necessary to run cars.

Make no mistake, the noise was deafening.

There WAS traffic on 30 Highway. No one dared look out the windows or move until permission was granted from the teacher, my Aunt Dale. She moved to the front of the room and slightly opened the door. All heads turned as she approached the door. The noise out on the gravel and sand highway grew increasingly loud.

I could feel my heart beating in my chest. At that very minute so many thoughts were going through my mind.

The German spy!

Had he come back and brought the whole German Army?

My brothers were both in the war, one in the Marines, the other in the Navy. I had gotten over some of my fear after moving into town where there were more people around. But this was Beat Two. This was the Keel Community and there should not have been any traffic like this on 30 Highway.

My mind completely ran away with me. My mind went back to the encounter with the German spy, when I escaped him by running between his legs and out the door of his pole cabin; then later in town, the encounter with him and the well dressed kid on the bicycle, what did all this mean?

I was really too scared to know exactly, then Aunt Dale threw the school door open, and when she did we could see Army soldiers, jeeps, trucks, tanks, and everything that I could imagine that the Army could fight with. There were hundreds of these soldiers and hundreds of Army vehicles, as far as you could see. They were coming from the direction of town.

Even in my fear, I could see the big white star on the vehicles. This was no mistake; every jeep, truck, tank, and cannon had a big white star on it, making it unmistakably identified as ours, the U.S.A.

Aunt Dale said to us, "Come and see."

There was a mad scramble for all ten or eleven of us to get a place where we could see what was happening.

Wow!

There were soldiers in combat gear, field packs, steel helmets, and rifles. They had it all.

They were here to train for combat, from the Army camp at Grenada, about fifty miles away. We learned later that as part of their training, they had been sent to participate in maneuvers, war games, in the nearby National Forest. After two weeks here, they would be sent across the ocean to either Europe or the Pacific to fight the war.

To fight the war over there so that it would not be fought here. Now I had a pretty good idea of what the spy was spying on. Either he wanted to learn about the Army or maybe he knew that they were keeping Japanese prisoners at a camp built at Como, only about forty miles away, or maybe he wanted to spy on the University's training command or maybe all of them.

When I realized that the soldiers were here, I had a warm feeling about having the security of the United States Army here to protect us. My brothers would take care of me, except they were away taking care of the business of the Navy and the Marines, who knows where.

"Road Guards out!"

shouted one of the soldiers who seemed to be in charge. At that instant two of the soldiers ran out and stopped the column of the advancing Army. One of them went over and opened a cattle gap in the barbed wire fence that would give access to the land beside the Keel School House.

"Column left!"

shouted the soldier in charge.

The whole Army turned left off 30 Highway, through the gap and into the school yard.

The jeep that was leading this group of soldiers came across the front of the school grounds and stopped at the front of our school. All of us kids were amazed at what we had seen. We were so excited that we could not speak.

By now Aunt Dale had ventured out of the schoolhouse and was standing in the yard with all of us kids behind her. The jeep that had stopped in the yard had a special driver; he stayed in the jeep and another man got out and came over to Aunt Dale. The man took off his helmet and began to speak to Aunt Dale. He was A polite and well mannered person and he explained that he and his people would be in the area for the next two weeks. In spite of being sweaty and dusty, he was nice and pleasant.

After a brief description of his plans, he told Aunt Dale that if any damage was done to the school property, she was to file papers with the Army at Camp McCain, near Grenada. As he gave her the papers, he turned, put on his helmet, and went back to his jeep. On the back of his helmet were two white bars, which was the only thing on his uniform that would show what rank he was.

One by one the vehicles turned into the pasture; about twenty five jeeps, some trucks, a tank, and even one ambulance made their way into the area. The people in charge directed every one of these people to the place that they wanted them to be. They set up a small tent back behind the school. The tent was just a piece of canvas without sides that gave a little bit of shelter from the sun. They put this tent in a clump of sweet gum trees out of sight of 30 Highway. The man with the two white bars on the back of his helmet ordered his jeep driver to move his belongings from the jeep into this tent.

After all of the trucks and tanks were put in place, the soldiers started to dig holes in places near the guns and tanks. Each man had his own hole. The holes were long enough that each person could lie down in it and deep enough so that they could hide in them. The dirt that came out of the holes was piled up around the edge to give more protection.

When dinner time came we did not get to go outside. The teacher said we must stay inside so that we did not bother the soldiers. I really believed that she was scared for us to be outside. I know I was excited because all of this was so new to me. I had never seen but one or two soldiers at one time and these were family friends home for a furlough. Now we had hundreds of soldier's right in our schoolyard.

I asked to be excused to go to the toilet. I knew that this would be the best chance to see the tanks and jeeps up close and I wanted to look into one of those holes that they had dug. Aunt Dale told me I could go to the toilet, but I had to wait since all of the boys would need to go at the same time.

Of course the girls always went to a different location and she would take the girls.

As we headed out in the direction of the boys toilet, we had to go by one of the guns, it was so big it was pulled by a truck. The soldiers spoke to us and we talked to them. I had planned and hoped that I would get a chance to see the soldiers up close. I really wanted to see the holes that they were digging. The soldiers called them fox-holes. The men were all friendly and showed us their rifles. I asked to see a hand grenade and one of them showed me one, explaining that it made smoke instead of an explosion. The bullets were "blanks", but they looked just like real bullets, except they had wax in the end. They would make a bang but were harmless as far as bullets are concerned.

We stayed too long, but I had spent enough time with the soldiers to decide that someday I wanted to be a soldier too. All this looked like so much fun. None of us boys really needed to go to the toilet; we had only used this for an excuse to be around the soldiers.

We could hear Aunt Dale calling us to come back, so we all ran back to the schoolhouse.

When we got back Aunt Dale dismissed school for the day. She decided we had had enough excitement and besides that, she didn't think we could learn much with all the confusion going on around us.

Aunt Dale usually walked to school along with all of the Williams children. They walked both to and from school, which was about three miles.

Today was different. Uncle Luther had come for us in his truck because of all the soldiers in the woods. We all piled into the truck and started up the rutted dirt road in the direction of the Williams place. The road eventually took us by Uncle Luther's house. This was the end of the road except for a field road that went across

Puss-Cuss Creek and then to the Cambridge Road. Most of this land was government land, except for the Williams' place and Uncle Luther's place.

The soldiers were in their places all along the road and well into the woods, as far as I could see. The ones that had been there long enough were so well hidden that it was hard to see them. The guns and tanks were covered with net that looked like chicken wire and had bushes and tree limbs covering them to hide them from sight.

I was glad that I was staying with the Williams kids because I knew Aunt Dale would not permit me to go outside once we got home.

When we got to the Williams' house, I got off the truck, got my bag with my extra clothes and started to the house. Aunt Dale asked me if I was sure I wanted to stay here with the Williams.

I was sure.

I loved Aunt Dale and Uncle Luther, but they were too protective of me. I needed to have a chance to see the soldiers up close. There were no soldiers on the land that belonged to the Williams. This was private land and the Army wanted the soldiers to stay on the National Forest land.

I was really in luck because the following day would be Saturday.

No school for two days! After we got our clothes changed, we grabbed a piece of cold corn bread and ran out to do the chores.

Mrs. Williams told the girls to stay away from the soldiers and told us boys to get on with the chores; "We all have to keep on living, even with all them soldiers around," she said.

We boys went right out the back door, down the path to the hog pen, and across to where the government land started. And just as we thought, there were the soldiers. They were "dug in," well hidden, in those fox holes. Some were still digging, some were arranging tree limbs and bushes to cover up the fresh dirt and to, as they said, break the lines of the big metal objects, making the guns, tanks, and trucks harder to be recognized by their shapes.

The soldiers who had their work done were sitting around; some were eating their supper. They seemed not to mind us watching them. They were friendly and talkative, and answered all of our questions. I could not think of much to say, although I had a lot of questions in my mind. I was somewhat bashful about starting a conversation with the soldiers.

The soldiers were eating food from small cans, I asked one of the soldiers what he was eating. He called it K-rations and C-rations. The C-rations were all in Army color cans that had its own opening key, a twist of the key and it was open. There was meat and gravy, beans; they even had crackers in those little cans. One had a chocolate bar in it. The food they called K-rations was dried food in packages, they would open a pack and pour in water and they would have peaches, milk, gravy, even soup. I had never seen food like that.

One of the soldiers asked me if I wanted a candy bar as he stirred white powder into water to make milk.

Then he asked if we had any real milk.

I said, "sure, sweet milk or butter milk?"

He said, "It don't matter."

He gave me a candy bar. I said I'd bring the milk later.

After we finished the chores we went to the spring house and carefully pulled up one of the small ropes that were hanging out of the water, each rope was attached to a large jar of milk. There were three ropes and three jugs of milk. We carefully took the rope off one of the gallon jugs, cold and wet from the cold spring water. The oldest Williams boy took the milk jug as we quickly went around to the kitchen and asked their mother if we could have some corn bread. She said, "I thought you boys had already had some bread when you came home from school." Someone in the crowd said, "Yes mam, but we just got two pieces." She said, "Go ahead and help your selves. I'm going to make hot bread for supper, anyway."

We very carefully took the five squares of corn bread left on the plate from dinner. I slid them off the plate so as to not drop them. We didn't have anything to wrap them in so I took the bread in my hands. I was appointed to carry the bread because my hands were the cleanest. We took off toward the soldiers with the jug of milk and the bread. We didn't even check to see if it was sweet or butter milk.

He said it didn't matter.

When we got to the place where we last saw the men in the group, the place where the one had asked for milk, we found most of the soldiers were sitting around eating supper. They were really happy to see us, they were especially proud to see what we had brought for them.

These people were just plain people like our families, except most were from other regions of the country. The one from New Jersey spoke with a different accent. One was from Missouri, and two were from East Tennessee, the area near the Smoky Mountains. These two were more like our country people, easy to talk to. One was named Robert Taylor and the other was James Harwell.

They were both in the State Militia and called into active service when the war started.

All these soldiers were so proud of the milk and bread.

I wonder about my brothers; I wonder if my brothers had any milk and bread or anything at all to eat. I wonder if my brothers even had a foxhole.

*****

My mind went back in time to another day when my brothers were cleaning the manure from the stables in our barn to be spread over our fields; this was always done before spring plowing began. This was not a haphazard operation, but one that required great planning and diligence.

They hitched up our team to the mule drawn wagon and placed it in the hall of the barn. They put on their black rubber knee boots and their oldest, most worn out work clothes.

They then began by scooping out the manure with shovels. This was a very smelly job at best, but it was usually done in the late winter, so the smell of manure was not as strong as, say, in July. This manure was loaded onto the wagon.

The wagon had a special "pole" bed, rigged up for this purpose. The poles were two by fours with the ends to the rear of the wagon rounded into handles so that the poles could be loosened from the rear as the wagon and team were driven across the filed. As the poles were loosened the manure fell through the cracks to the ground to enrich the corn field. The wagon moved up and another pole loosened and the manure spread across the soon-to-be-plowed-field. This process continued until the stables were cleaned out and the field was covered with a thin application of manure. Daddy would fertilize the corn fields with manure but he used bought fertilizer for his cotton, his cash crop.

After my brothers finished hauling manure to the field, we decided that we would drive the wagon and team across the shallow part of the pond in order to wash the wagon and free it of the excess manure that had collected underneath the pole bed.

As the team headed into the water something scared the mules, causing them to shy away and head across the deep part of the pond. As the water got deeper, the mules started to swim. After getting in the deeper water, the two by four poles floated off the wagon. One of my brothers jumped off and took me with him. He told me to grab onto the two by four poles that he had floated over to me. I grabbed the poles and hung on for dear life. He grabbed onto a large group of poles that would support his weight. We floated. My other brother stayed with the wagon and somehow was able to hang on and drive the swimming team of mules out of the water to safety on the other side of the stock pond.

After we finally got out of the water we realized how frightened we were. We were safe, but wet and cold. We weren't scared of anything in particular, except my brothers could not swim, neither could I. I was grateful that my brothers had protected me and kept me safe in the deep water. The day was not especially cold but it was early spring and our wet clothes made us shiver. We huddled around each other trying to decide what to do.

My brothers decided that their old worn-out, manure-stained clothes would be thrown away after today's work, so they would bathe and change into fresh clothes. But my clothes were not to be thrown away. I was not dirty with manure, only wet and cold from the wagon-washing experience.

One of my brothers sneaked quietly into the house and got me a set of clean dry clothes and my other shoes, and brought them to me. We all changed into our dry clothes and my brothers hung my wet clothes in the barn, out of sight, to dry and later to be washed on wash day. They threw away their old worn-out, wet clothes. Nothing was ever said about the incident.

As long as my parents lived, neither of them ever knew how well my brothers had protected and taken care of me. It remained our secret.

*****

I woke up and thought, it is Saturday, no school. While the Williams boys were doing the morning chores, I ran down by the hog pen and over to where the soldiers were camped.

To my surprise they were breaking camp and getting ready to

move out. They said that they were moving to a place that was near Riverside. They were practicing setting up and moving out. The soldiers who were so nice to me and the Williams boys gave me a whole duffel bag full of stuff, with K-Rations and C-Rations. There was a whole box of blank bullets and another box of blank bullets that had been shot, empty hulls the Williams boys called them. I could not carry this big bag. I took the strap and dragged it out of the area where the fox holes were dug, trying to get out of their way.

I was standing there looking at the different things that were happening and all the different directions that everybody was going. It was total confusion but everybody had his own job to do and in a short time everybody was finished, soon they were in their jeeps and trucks and ready to move out.

The soldier from Tennessee, Robert Taylor, ran by and squatted down beside me. He said he really appreciated me bringing the milk and patted me on the back as he walked away. I thought about my brothers.

I watched as the last jeep pulled out; they were gone in such a short time and left nothing but some partially filled fox holes. I hardly had a chance to say anything, but I would like to have had a chance to say good-by. There was a strange attachment to some of the soldiers, like I had known them for a long time. I guess maybe it was because we were all country boys.

I dragged the duffel bag as far as I could. It was stuffed completely full. I left it under a large cedar tree well hidden. I don't know why I hid the bag; no one would possibly find it except one of the Williams family. Nevertheless I hid the bag until we could come back for it with enough help to carry it up the hill to the house. When we finally got a good chance to bring the big duffel bag up to the barn where we could examine its contents we were surprised to find such an assortment of military treasures.

Besides the rations there were first aid packs for each of us, salt tablets, and little tablets to purify drinking water. The soldiers had really fixed us up. There was a large knapsack with straps on it so that I could wear it on my back like a field pack. There was a note for me, and it said I hope you enjoy the stuff.

I hope you never have to use anything like this.

Thanks for the butter milk. It was signed Bob Taylor.

Chapter 19

The Studio

Louie asked me if I would help him do an odd job on Saturday. We went to his grandmother's house across town on Mill Street. We got there early and Granny Parsons was in the kitchen fixing breakfast for us. I had already had breakfast earlier, but I couldn't resist the plate of pancakes she set in front of me; they looked so good, golden brown. Louie ate his pancakes with butter and syrup and almost swallowed them whole. I was not so hungry so I made mine last a little longer. The chocolate milk finished off a great breakfast.

We were there to clean and take out rubbish from the studio apartment upstairs. Louie's grandmother had rented the small apartment to a new professor at the University. The housekeeper's studio had sat empty and collected junk since it had become vacant. Granny Parson's invalid sister had died, so there was no reason for the housekeeper to stay on.

Louie's grandpa Parsons had died long before Louie could remember him. Granny Parsons had continued to live here on Mill Street across from the Ole Miss Campus, where his grandpa had taught chemistry for a number of years. Granny Parsons could use the extra money from the rented apartment.

Only the railroad tracks separated this street from the campus.

We had made hundreds of trips from upstairs down to the corner where the refuse was to await the garbage collection truck which would come by on Monday.

Louie and I had worked all morning moving, sweeping and mopping the floor. Granny Parsons had directed each part of the activity, we were finished with the work and now we were ready for lunch. Granny Parsons had us go out on the screened back porch to wait for lunch. Louie was in a hammock and I was lying on a big rug on the floor. From where I was, I could see the front of the house and I noticed a man coming up the walk to the house. He was dressed up.

I could not believe my eyes.

Yes!

It was the strange looking man with the well dressed kid. The last time I had seen them they were at my Mama's front door. Here he was again, wearing the same suit, tie and hat. But now the kid had on ordinary looking clothes; today he was dressed like any other boy with shirt, pants and tennis shoes.

I looked hard to be sure that the people were really who I thought them to be.

It was them!

Why was that kid here?

The kid that almost ran over Lillian Bost.

Lillian Bost!

Oh! No time now to think about how pretty Lillian Bost was. That would take a long, long time.

I grabbed Louie by the arm and made a sign to keep him quiet. I motioned to him that he should look to the front of the house. Louie looked in disbelief. He whispered in agreement, that this was the same pair that we had seen at the Doolittle house. The last time we had seen them, the boy was putting the bicycle in the garage, and he was all dressed up in that Sunday school suit.

What did all of this mean? I did not know.

One thing I did know; I did not want them to see me right now, not until I had time to think.

Granny Parsons called, "Louie, come here."

I didn't wait.

I ran out the back door, rolled down the kudzu covered bank and ended up on the railroad track that bordered the University Campus, and ran desperately toward the University Bridge. I was running so hard my side hurt. I had to get to the bridge, a place to hide. I finally reached the place where University Avenue crosses over the railroad track. I wanted to sit down, but had to lie down in order to catch my breath. At this point I was not sure if I had been seen by the two renters.

Louie did not know anything about my encounter with the spy in his pole cabin on 30 Highway.

I had told him about the two coming to Mama's boarding house and inquired about renting rooms, after we had seen them at the Doolittle's house. But now the spy was still our secret, just Gracie's and mine.

I would have told him the story, but I had sworn secrecy to Gracie from the very first day that she showed me the hideout. I didn't know how soon I would be able to see Gracie to get her permission to talk about our secret. Then I could tell Louie. But Louie's Granny is renting her studio apartment to German Spies.

Now!

Oh boy, what a mess.

Where does loyalty stop and better judgment begin?

Besides, I could not prove that they are spies, and neither could Louie.

After I was able to breathe again, I could think a little clearer. I knew I needed to get to my house and the quickest way was to go up the railroad, past the depot, and up the long hill to the square, then one more block to Mama's boarding house. I ran all the way home without stopping.

When I ran up the steps and into the house, Mama and Aunt Polly had just finished shelling a whole bushel of peas, big, plump, purple hulled peas, the kind that would turn your fingers purple for at least two days and everybody would know at a glance that you had been relegated to domestic housework.

My Aunt Polly said to me, half laughing, "Where have you been? Is somebody chasing you? Are you in trouble?"

I replied, "No, I don't think so".

I was not sure, but I wasn't about to say anything more.

Mama said for me to get a trash can and take the pea hulls out for the garbage. As I was taking the trash out, it was going through my mind that all day I have taken stuff to the street for the garbage truck to pick up on Monday.

Up the steps and down the steps, and out with the trash. As I neared the street curb, I looked both ways, checking, to see if the spies might be in the neighborhood. They have a strange way of turning up, almost as if they are following me.

I put the trash on the curb and ran back up the steps.

Mrs. Parsons came by our house on Monday and left money for me for helping with the clean up of the studio apartment. She asked Mama why I ran away before she got lunch finished. Mama didn't know anything about the incident so she could not answer.

Granny Parsons left me two dollars and fifty cents for working that Saturday morning. That was more than I had ever earned. I had a dollar that I had earned mowing a neighbors grass.

I went that very day to the Morgan and Lindsey Store and bought three dollars and fifty cents worth of war stamps. They cost ten cents each and I would lick them and stick them in a book. The book held eighteen dollars and seventy five cents worth of war stamps. When the book was filled I would take it back to Morgan Lindsey's and they would exchange it for a twenty five dollar war bond. This money went to the government to help pay for the war; eighteen dollars and seventy five cents would be worth twenty five dollars in ten years. And the government bought jeeps, trucks, planes, bandages, guns, K-rations, and even uniforms. Scrap metal, scrap paper, scrap aluminum were saved for the war effort. I took everything that I could save for the scrap drive to school and turned it in. I got a credit slip every time I gave something. To me, it was a thank you note from a soldier.

Chapter 20

Assembly

One day at Oxford Elementary School there was an unexpected school-wide assembly. There were many surprise assemblies there, because the principal loved to sing. On some occasions he would impulsively call an assembly. All students would gather in the auditorium where he would be alone on the stage of the auditorium, just him and the grand piano. Song sheets were handed out and we would sing for an hour. I learned that the sixth grades were always seated in the balcony area, away from the rest of the lower grades; quite a status symbol.

Just think, sitting up in the balcony, looking down on the lowly first, second, third, fourth and fifth grades.

Two more years.

Something to look forward to.

But today it would be different. The girl that I had seen when Mama enrolled me in the fourth grade, the girl with the long pig tails, read the assembly announcement.

This would different, very different.

No singing today; this would be an exciting event. We would be part of a special recognition. At the appointed time, we were told by the teacher to file out single file down the hall, down the steps past the music room and past the huge display cases that lined both sides of the entrance hall.

Outside!

We would have an outside assembly!

The first, second and third grades were already there, neat rows of students arranged along the long front steps next to the sidewalk, then we added to the group and shortly afterward the fifth and sixth grades were lined up behind us.

I had never seen such a gathering. A policeman and another man had stopped traffic on Jackson Avenue. There was a big Army truck parked on the gravel parking lot across the street, and soldiers were taking a jeep out of the truck. They had ramps from the back of the truck, and they were carefully backing the jeep out and down the ramps. The truck and jeep were just exactly like the ones I had seen up close on the maneuvers at Keel School last year. There were three soldiers working and two important looking men watching. One of the important-looking men was a General.

Wow!

A General!

A real General.

His uniform was different from the men doing the work. He had one star on his hat and one star on each of his shoulders.

When the jeep was parked at a spot just as he wanted it, the General came to the front of the assembly, and called for our school principle to come forward.

The two men shook hands and the General gave our school principal a paper and made a short speech. He was recognizing our school for bringing in enough scrap material and war stamps and bonds to have enough money to pay for a jeep.

Wow; we had bought a jeep!

What an achievement!

What a big payoff.

Our school had paid for a jeep; in dollars and cents I don't know how much it was, it doesn't matter. We had produced enough money and material, and a bunch of kids had bought a jeep.

At the end of the short speech we were allowed to file by the jeep and each of us could touch it if we wanted to. I really had a good feeling inside, I was proud to be a part of this group of students. I loved Keel School but this would be one of the greatest experiences of my life.

We had bought a jeep that soldiers like Robert Taylor and James Harwell could ride in.

Chapter 21

The Night Marshal

Now I have to make a decision. I promised Gracie that I would keep my word, but I couldn't stand by and let German spies move into Louie's granny's studio apartment.

What a deal!

Gracie would have to understand.

Besides, the spies were are no longer a threat to Gracie; they were in my neighborhood now.

I would do it.

I would tell Louie without Gracie's permission.

I would wait until I was sure Louie was home from his Granny's; then I would go across my back yard to Louie's house. I didn't want to go in the front door because the pair of spies still lived at the Doolittle's house across from Louie.

I told Louie the whole story, word for word.

Louie exclaimed in a shout, "I don't believe it; that dressed up kid, a spy!"

He did believe it too, I knew he did.

A Spy! He almost ran over Lillian Bost on that black bicycle.

"Spies don't belong in Oxford, We've got to do something," Louie said.

He could figure out some of the answers. Together, with our knowledge of the Dick Tracy stuff, we were able to fill in all the blanks.

Neither Louie nor I knew what to do, but we knew we had to do something.

Louie and I had been best friends since I moved to Oxford and he took a part in my fight with the tough town boys. Now he would step in and help me again.

We did not know anything about spies, except what we had read in our Dick Tracy comic books and what we had seen in the Saturday movie serials at the Ritz Theater.

Louie said he knew of a policeman that we could talk to. He did not know him personally but he knew that he was the husband of the lady who runs the lunchroom at school.

Maybe we could talk to her and she could get him to do something. I had never eaten in the lunchroom, I asked for money to eat there. Mama gave me the fifteen cents it took to eat lunch. It was Friday and I would be able to see what smelled so good on Fridays. The lunchroom had good smells coming from it every day. It was located right next to our school in a part of the old abandoned Oxford High School building. All that was left of that old school building was the part used for our lunchroom and another room where the safety patrol stored bikes for the students that rode bicycles to school.

Friday's smells were special; all the kids knew the smell of spaghetti and home made rolls. Ooooh, it smelled sooo good. I had never eaten spaghetti. It was not something we grew on our farm, so the smell was strange to me, but wonderfully delicious.

We had already paid for our lunch in our room at school. That was the first order of business after roll call. The lunchroom lady was checking names at her desk at the door.

While I was waiting in line, I could see Lillian Bost, she was so pretty, so pretty that I just stood there and looked at her. "Move on up", said a boy as he pushed me from behind. I hadn't realized the line had moved because I was looking at Lillian Bost, the prettiest girl I had ever seen.

When we moved up and Louie got to the desk, he spoke quietly to the lady and told her we needed to talk to her husband, the night marshal of the town.

She thought that we were in some kind of trouble but Louie convinced her that we only needed to get his advice about a problem with a dog. He had lied to her. Louie had lied in order to help me out. She told us to come by their house after school. The marshal would be awake at that time and getting ready to go to work at five o'clock for the night shift.

The night marshal lived on the same street that I did, so I decided I had to go to Louie's, and cut through his neighbor's yard so Mama would not see us. We came out in the back yard of the night marshal. We went to the back door and knocked.

When he came to the door, I thought he was a giant. He was a very large man, about six feet and six inches tall. His shoulders were the widest I have ever seen. His waist was small, so small he had to have wide suspenders to hold up his pants. His body filled up the opening of the door. I was sure glad he was Louie's friend.

He said "come on in boys," in his deep voice. His words nearly shook the roof. He was such a huge, strong man. I was sure glad he was on our side. I hoped he would be, anyway.

When we went in, he sat in a large rocking chair and we sat on the couch. He said in his booming voice, "what kind of problem do you boys have?"

When Louie introduced me, the marshal asked me my father's name. He said he had heard that my father had died and that he was very sorry. He said that he had been in the Army with Daddy in France, in another war.

We tried to find a good place to start, and finally got around to starting with Gracie taking me to the pole cabin.

I had already told two people the secret Gracie and I had promised to keep, but because of the war effort, I could justify my action. Beside that, the spy was in my neighborhood now.

Gracie would understand.

She would just have to.

I believed she would.

After telling the whole story the marshal stood up. He was such a tall, strong man. In his loud booming voice he said, "boys, something will have to be done about this, but I'm not sure what." At that time he questioned me again about the radios and the books I had described that were under the spy's bed in the pole cabin.

"Are you sure they are German," he asked?

"I don't know," I said. They looked like German to me, but I had never seen a German or a German book. I really believed that they were. I wished I knew as much as Dick Tracy did, then I would know for sure about the books and if they were really German. But I'm not Dick Tracy and so I just have to wonder about all of this.

The marshal seemed to be sure about one thing; we needed help. He thought we needed to start with Mama.

Since it was getting late she would wonder where I was. As we went out the front door, the marshal asked if my Mama knew about any of this.

I said "no"!

He said, "She's got to be told."

I said, "no, she won't understand!"

He said, "boy's this is war time, she will understand". We sat down with Mama and I re-told the story all up to date, right up to today.

He was right, she did understand. From that day on he was my friend; just like Louie, he was defending me. They were doing what my brothers would have done to protect me.

The next day was Saturday. The Marshal came to the boarding house on Saturday afternoon. He had a man with him named Winfred Jackson. He wore a suit and a hat. When Mama invited the two men into the living room, Mr. Jackson got out a black identification folder with his badge. It said he was an F.B.I Agent.

I nearly swallowed my teeth; a real F.B.I man! A G-man!

He did not even look like Dick Tracy, which I was sure all F.B.I people would look like. Mr. Jackson had been given the story by the night marshal, but he said he needed to get the complete story from me and Gracie.

WOAH!

Gracie.

Gracie did not even know that I had told anyone about our secret. Boy this really changed things around.

What was I to do?

We all talked about it and the night marshal said in his loud booming voice, "son, you don't really have a choice, this thing is bigger than all of us here. A whole lot bigger.

She will understand, just like your Mama did."

The night marshal was wise. He had dealt with people for a great many years, some bad, mostly good, but he knew exactly what he was talking about.

*****

Gracie did understand just as he said she would. The law people had allowed me to talk to Gracie alone for a few minutes.

They had a plan all worked out. After all, G-men always had a plan; they had all kind of experience in such matters. We had all been asked to meet in the courtroom of the city hall, Gracie and her parents, Mama and me, Louie and his parents and his Granny.

After the night marshal started, he came right to the point, "I'm not sure what all we have here, but we need expert help." He explained that the potential for disaster was very great, there was even a possibility that lives could be at risk. With the war effort and the spy question, we had to be very careful. He could have taken over and run the show, but he had given the leadership over to the G-Men.

So, the plan would be carried out by Mr. Jackson, the F.B.I. man.

Mr. Jackson spoke quietly and right to the point. The plan was to permit the strangers to move right into the studio apartment as they had planned. Dangerous, yes, but he pledged complete protection for Granny Parsons and he let us all know that we were not to discuss any of this plan with each other and certainly not anyone else outside this room. The plan was simple. We all had to keep our mouth shut and let the G-men work their plan; otherwise, it could mean disaster. We would be contacted only if we were needed.

A few days later I was at Louie's house after school to study. We were on his front porch and just as plain as day, there they were, the two spies, loading their stuff in the back of a panel truck. I don't know how long they had been working when we got there, but they were finished and away from the Doolittle place in only a few minutes.

Louie said the truck they were using was one owned by the

wholesale grocery company at the depot. They used this small truck to deliver small orders of groceries and sometimes they rent out the truck and the driver, by the hour.

We had a pretty good idea where they were moving, but we took off across town to Mill Street to see for ourselves. When we got to Louie's grandmother's house, the panel truck was backed up to the side entrance of the front porch. The two men and the boy were busy taking boxes into the house, up the stairs to the studio apartment.

Louie and I ran across the side yard and into the

screened back porch and, into the kitchen. Louie's Granny was sitting down at the kitchen table looking real worried. She was glad to see us. She hugged us both. Granny Parsons offered to get us some milk and cookies, which we gratefully accepted, as we were always hungry after school. She said, "boys, I hope this is the right thing to do."

The move was finished and the panel truck was away in hardly more than half and hour. We could hear muffled sounds from upstairs as the renters walked about and arranged their belongings.

What else could they be doing? With all of that radio stuff, they could be doing just about anything.

Chapter 22
Exit

The week came and went. Louie and his Granny came back from church Sunday morning and there was not a sound in the house. Granny Parsons said usually there could be heard some sounds coming from upstairs in the studio apartment. Not today. We wondered if maybe they too had gone to church or just out. Somewhere spying.

But who knows. As the day went on, a careful watch by Granny Parsons revealed nothing. Night-time came, no trace of the renters. What could have become of the new residents?

Granny Parsons said she had not heard a sound, from them since she went to bed on Saturday night around ten o'clock. We were curious that not a sound had been heard from them in nearly thirty-six hours. I was staying the night with Louie and his Granny to be around there if help were needed, really only to reassure each other.

Monday morning a truck drove into the drive way followed by a car, the car was driven by the G-Man, Mr. Jackson. He had another man with him, whom he did not introduce to us. Neither did he introduce the two men in the truck. Mr. Johnson spoke briefly with Granny Parsons.

The men went up the stairs and entered the studio. In an instant they started bringing down the belongings of the strange-looking bicycle riders. Box by box they brought the stuff down.

The government man and his helpers kept a list of each item. The helper stayed at the truck and directed the loading.

There was the big green box that looked like a big radio; there was the raincoat and the cap that I had seen hanging in the pole cabin.

There was another larger package; it was a radio, even larger than the ones I had seen in the hide-out behind Gracie's house. The two men from the truck kept bringing more stuff down. It became evident that the two renters had moved in much more stuff than I had seen in the pole cabin hide-out on 30 highway.

The F.B.I. was finished, gone, and with them all hopes of ever knowing any more about these two strange people and their plans. Where were the renters? What could possibly have happened to them?

The G-Men knew.

I was sure they did.

But they were not saying.

Just like they told us. We had to be quiet about the whole thing. We had sworn.

Louie and I ran to the top of the stairs and looked into the studio. There was nothing at all to show for this whole experience. Every foot of the apartment was bare. We were really disappointed and yet, we were somewhat relieved.

When we started to go downstairs, I felt something strange under the linoleum near the corner by the bedroom door. I felt the slight bulge and there was something under the rug that felt like a newspaper. I showed it to Louie. We very carefully lifted the corner of the rug. It wasn't a newspaper, it was one of the radio code manuals open like a magazine, to the middle and flattened out, and stuffed under the linoleum rug. There was the design of the Iron Cross on the back just as I had seen months before on that hot day that I had first explored the stranger's cabin.

I could not believe it, Louie's eyes got big and we both were breathless from the excitement.

The very same book that I had discovered on an earlier time; Not a word could I read, only recognizing the Iron Cross the symbol of the German spies, according to Dick Tracy and his G-Men.

Louie knew in a second what it was by my description. We talked quietly, as quietly as we could keep ourselves. We did not know what we should do with the book. Finally, we decided that I should keep the book with the Iron Cross on the back, since it was I that first found it. But what if it was hidden in a moment of desperation as the spies were being discovered? What if the spies had left it purposely and another spy would come back looking for it?

What if the government men left it as bait to see who they would catch next?

I wondered where my brothers were.

Printed in the United States
54200LVS00001B/180

9 781596 820890